To c

Kay & / on.

Enjoy.

THE PIER

Frank

By: Frank L Anastasio Jr

THIS BOOK IS DEDICATED

TO

ALL THOSE WHO ENJOY READING

ACTION ROMANTIC MYSTERIES

It is curious that physical courage should be so common in the world and moral courage so rare.

Mark Twain

OTHER BOOKS BY

FRANK L ANASTASIO JR

The Adventures of I.A.N.

An Indelible Psyche (The Dork)

Beyond the Clouds

The Dance of the Mockingbird

The Astonishing Chronicle of our Amazing Ancestors

PART ONE

Day of The Incident

CHAPTER ONE

The Incident on the Pier
Saturday, March 23, 2013 at 9:42 AM

From the end of the pier, a scream pierces the still cold air; a scream that identifies pure terror and horror and fear; a scream that stops all activities.

"Help! . . . Help! . . . That man just pushed a little girl over the rail! Help somebody! . . . Help! . . . He threw that little girl over! Stop him! Get him! . . . Help her somebody! . . . Help her!"

Twelve Minutes Earlier At 9:30 AM

In the cold waters below the Gulf Pier, a giant shadowy form slowly skims inches above the white sandy bottom. Frustrated in its hunt for an unwary blue crab, sting ray, or flounder, the menacing undulating shadow rises gradually toward the surface in search of other prey. Above the pier, occasional rays of brilliant sun streak through the generally overcast sky bringing temporary warmth to the eager anglers and curious visitors.

The mid March wintry winds that moved through yesterday morning have died to a complete calm. Only slight swells on the surface of the icy Gulf of Mexico can be perceived. This virtually smooth surface allows everyone to see down several feet into the limpid emerald green water. Numerous fishermen, both local and tourist, have gathered on the pier in hopes of catching a meal for the evening. In truth, only those who have learned the correct techniques and possess the proper gear required to fish from the giant pier, have much chance at success. The experienced locals have staked their claim to their 'ideal location' on the octagon shaped end of the pier where the seafloor is nearly thirty feet below the surface.

Frequent local visitors, Samuel Walker and his son David casually stroll and observe the various activities as they make their way to the pier's busy end. Stopping along the way they watch a young fisherman bring up several pin fish caught in his brightly colored monofilament trap. Samuel Walker explains to David that he will use the pin fish as live bait to catch a much larger fish. David nods that he understands and scurries to another fisherman to ask him about his gear. After getting a satisfying answer he turns and notices another man, but this one is only carrying a large round net with a coiled black nylon rope attached. He finds that interesting. He runs up to him and asks, "Hey Mister. What are you going to do with that net and rope? It's huge! You don't even have a pole. You think you can just scoop them up with that?"

The man pauses and laughs out loud. He stoops down to be at eye level and answers, "No, big guy, I don't fish. I just like to watch. I just bring my net in case somebody catches a really big one. Then they'll use the net to hoist it up from the water to the deck," he explains.

"Oh!" he says, satisfied with the answer. He turns and darts off to check out another fisherman who appears, judging by the extreme bend in his pole, to be reeling in something big.

Ten minutes pass and Mr. Walker and David have only made it a little more than halfway to the long pier's end. They pause and turn their interest to something that other visitors seem to have spotted in the waters below. David scampers ahead and jumps on the bottom board of the guardrail. He stretches over the top rail as far as he can and shouts excitedly, "Come see Dad! It's a shark! Wow! Look at him! He's huge! Look Dad, look! What kind is it?"

"I'm not sure," his dad answers as he grabs hold of David's belt while carefully leaning over the guardrail himself. He stares down and studies the giant fish as it swims lazily beneath the pier.

A nearby elderly fisherman, baiting a hook for his next cast, overhears David and casually glances down. He declares, with an all knowing tone, "Oh, that's a bull shark. They are really aggressive. Son, you had better step down from that rail. You don't want to fall in and be eaten."

"I'm not going to fall in because I'm seven years old. . . . How big is he Mister?" David asserts and sternly asks.

"Oh, I'd say that-there fellow is seven to eight foot long. He's a big one. You're just the right size to be a good and tasty mouthful," he laughs.

David and his dad, along with several others, watch the shark for another ten minutes or so as it aggressively chomps down on wounded pin fish thrown in by the visitors.

Then the screams pierce the air. David jumps down from the rail and turns toward the mayhem. He can't make out what actually is being shouted by the frenzied crowd. As he strains to hear he gasps and retreats against the rail as he notices a long haired disheveled man appear out of the chaos and run directly toward him. The man seems to hesitate slightly as he glances down at David but continues sprinting toward the parking lot as he notices Mr. Walker. David follows the man's dash to get off the pier only briefly before turning his attention back to the uproar. He spots another man who seems to be hurriedly shedding his cap, jacket and shirt. He watches as he kicks off his shoes and is amazed as that man vaults himself over the rail and into the waters twenty feet below. Seconds later he sees one of the fishermen quickly pick up and toss over the round scoop net. David returns to his spot on the rail and again stretches out as far as he can to watch the rescue efforts going on below. He sees a small girl struggling to stay above water and a man hurriedly swimming to reach her.

A reflex reaction causes David to shout and point, "There she is! She's right in front of you! Look Dad, he almost has her!"

"I see!"

The rescuer approaches the girl from behind. She doesn't see him as he reaches out for her just as it appears she is sinking below the surface. Using powerful leg kicks he manages to place the struggling little girl into the net. She's immediately hauled to the deck shivering, screaming, and crying with fear but apparently unharmed. Several care-givers comfort her as the man momentarily treads water below. After a very quick look up to check on her he begins swimming toward the beach. David figures the man knows he's much too heavy for the rescue net.

The fishermen all applaud, as does David and his dad. The hero doesn't see it but everyone on the pier is bending over the railing and giving him a big thumbs-up.

David watches his efforts as his dad tells him that he should not have any trouble reaching shore because he looks like he's a real strong swimmer. David steps down and begins to run to see the little girl and to join in the excitement at the end of the pier. His dad reaches out and grabs him by his shirt collars and orders, "Oh, no you don't! You stay with me, young man. Lots of people are taking care of her and they don't need you in the way."

Suddenly there's another scream. This time it's from a woman who is standing right next to them. "The shark! The shark is after that young man!" she shouts. They all turn back to the guardrail and look over. . . . "And look! . . . Oh my God! . . . Look! There's a second one over there!"

Their hearts pound as they see the dorsal fin of the first giant shark pierce the surface only five or six yards behind the splashing feet of the swimmer. Trying desperately to alert him, everyone, including David and his dad, scream out as they point; "Shark! Watch out! A shark has seen you! Swim son swim! Swim fast Mister!"

"Oh my goodness! The second one is gaining on him too!" the woman screams again.

The young swimmer cannot hear anything except his exhaling bubbles and the gurgling of the cold water as it encircles and covers his ears. All watch in horror as the approaching fin moves in closer before sinking below the surface. Samuel Walker jerks his son back from the rail and orders him to look away. David turns and quickly buries his head against his dad as Mr. Walker pulls him in tightly.

CHAPTER TWO

Fifteen Minutes After the Incident
Saturday, March 23, 2013 at 10:15 AM

Justin Webb quickly jumps into his filthy, red-clay stained, 1984 Buick Regal. After frantically searching each of his pockets for his keys he nervously inserts them into the ignition and starts the engine. The exhaust initially belches a blue-white cloud that subsides as he drives quickly, but not conspicuously, toward busy Gulf Shores where he's eager to mingle with the many Spring Break vacationers and souvenir shoppers. After carefully avoiding onrushing police cruisers, ambulances, and fire trucks, he continues on to Daisy's Coffee Shop. He knows that several tourists were going to be having a late morning breakfast at this small and welcoming neighborhood restaurant. He brushes his unkempt long dirty blond hair out of his face and ties it back into a pony tail. He removes his blue jean jacket, throws it in the back seat, and grabs his sweat stained Braves baseball cap. Nervously pulling it down tightly on his head, he enters the restaurant.

"Hey, young fellow! What's all that commotion about out there?" an elderly gentleman shouts outs as he enters.

All heads turn first toward the gentleman then quickly to Justin Webb. They momentarily pause their eating while awaiting a comment.

Justin is startled that a question has been directed to him. He stares, with contempt, at the gentleman and glances quickly around the restaurant and answers, in a 'why-ask-me' loud voice, "Hell, I don't know. I was just driving along when all these damn cop cars fly pass me. Scared the crap out of me and damn near ran me off the road."

Satisfied with his response, he pulls out one of the chairs at a small round table that's located near the entrance. He gives the seat a quick brushing with the other hand and sits down as a waitress approaches. Smiling, she says to him, "Welcome Sir, welcome to Daisy's. If you don't mind, this table is taken. The gentleman at the buffet bar is sitting here. Would you mind switching to that table in the corner? You've arrived just in time, it's our last available."

"I don't see anybody sitting here. Why the hell should I move? . . . If the buffet guy was sitting here, tell the buffet guy to move," he barks.

Pausing at the shock of his comment, she says, "Sir, that's his coffee and I'm sure that he would like to finish it with his breakfast."

"Well move the damn coffee, and the cup, and the saucer to that other table! Then come back and wipe this one off and the problem is solved," he insists rudely with a mocking grin.

"Sir, please. We don't want a scene. Could you just move or I will have to call the manager over," she begs in a calm voice. She glances over and sees that the manager is indeed keeping one eye on the situation.

"You can call anybody you want lady!" he exclaims loudly.

The elderly gentleman, who has been listening to the conversation, stands and shouts, "Hey asshole! Get your scrawny, boney behind out of that chair and move to the other table as the nice waitress lady asked!"

"Shut the hell up old man! You and what army is going to make me?"

Just then the gentleman, three other male patrons, and one gray haired lady noisily slide their chairs back, stand and start moving toward Justin Webb.

"Whoa! Slow down! I didn't mean anything by what I said. I didn't want everybody to get upset. I'm out of here. I can't have no trouble with you old bastards. All I wanted was a glass of stupid water anyway. I don't want no trouble," he shouts as he darts toward the door.

"What an idiot!" the gentleman says. The others nod their heads in agreement as they return to their breakfast.

Many of the patrons keep an eye on him through the restaurant's large windows as he makes his way to his car.

+ + + +

Justin Webb sits for a second, tapping his fingernails on the steering wheel. Suddenly he explodes and starts pounding it with his bare palms. He stops a second and then begins anew, but this time punching the dusty dashboard with his closed fist.

"Look at that idiot!" the gentleman calls out. "He's been hitting and punching the dash and now it looks like he's talking to himself."

"Damn old farts. They nearly blew my cover," he mutters to himself as he roots through the glove compartment for his lighter and that half joint he's been saving. Finding and clipping it to a hairpin found under the brake pedal, he nervously lights up after placing it between his trembling lips. He inhales deeply and allows the smoke to penetrate totally into his lungs. "I went in there in the first place just so I would blend in with a dumb crowd; any dumb crowd. All I'm trying to do is fit in and not stand out in any way and those old bastards and that waitress bitch start causing trouble. Trouble I can't afford. I have to blend in. I have to be just one in a crowd. . . . Damn old farts."

Feeling the effects of the weed kick in, he ceases the pounding, punching, and talking to himself but before starting the car he slowly inspects his hands and fists. His palms are nearly beet red as are his knuckles. He flexes his left hand and loosely grabs his right wrist. He begins to slide the hand toward his elbow as he stares at his forearm and wonders why he's built so slim. Pumping weights and eating the so-called 'right things' has yielded nothing. Justin Webb stands about five feet ten and in all twenty-three of his years he's never been able to weigh more than one-thirty-five.

"I have to go see my sweet lady!" he says while angrily turning the key. "She'll be proud of me."

CHAPTER THREE

Forty-five Minutes After the Incident
Saturday, March 23, 2013 at 10:45 AM

"Okay, everybody step back and let the emergency rescue people tend to the girl," orders Detective Steven Acer.

Walking over to a young lady who he figures might be her mother he says, "Ma'am, I'm Detective Acer. Are you by any chance a relative of or acquainted with the little girl?"

"No. No I'm not. I've never seen her before. I was just hanging out on the pier; trying to catch some rays. I'm not having much luck though," she answers as she stares at this ruggedly handsome officer. She gives him the once-over and figures he's six one and around one hundred and ninety pounds. "A real hunk," she thinks.

"You were fishing?" Detective Acer asks.

"No; sun rays. Not sting rays," she says looking at him as if it's a shame that he doesn't have the brains to go along with the brawn.

"Were you here when it happened? Do you feel up to answering any questions if you were?"

"Sure; I was sitting right here. What would you like to know? I screamed by head off."

"What's your name and how old are you? That's just for the record," he asks.

"Susan Peters. I'm twenty-three. My friends call me Sunshine," she says as she brushes her long blond hair out of her face.

"I'm sure they do. Can you tell me what you saw, Ms. Peters?"

"It's Miss; Miss Susan Peters," she corrects.

Just then, one of the emergency personnel approaches the two and says, "Detective, I thought that you would like to know that the little girl said her name is Abby James and she lives somewhere 'not too far from here.' She didn't know the name of her hometown. She could be from out of town, but a town or city close by."

"Thanks. We'll start running her parents down. It shouldn't be too hard to find them. Thanks again." Returning to Miss Peters he says, "Sorry. I was asking you what you saw."

"Do you think her father could be the one who threw her over? That is unthinkable to me!" she exclaims.

"I have no idea, Miss Peters."

"I hope you catch the idiot."

"We will. Now can you tell me what you saw?"

"Well, this sleazy looking guy and the little girl were just walking around looking at the different catches that the fishermen had discarded and let die on the deck. He was holding her hand the whole time. She seemed like she knew him. She was really excited; especially when one fisherman allowed her to touch the eyeball of a big old dead fish. That sent a shiver down my spine." She pauses and gives her shoulders a quick shake as if the shiver has returned.

"Yes, Ma'am. Can you tell me about the man?" he asks.

"That's what I'm getting to. Stop interrupting me," she scolds and stares at him a second.

"Sorry? . . . The man, Miss Peters?"

"Like I was saying, I watched them as he walked around holding her hand. He was laughing and entertaining her. She loved it. All of a sudden he picks her up and sits her on the rail. I thought that was sort of risky so I kept watching. He was standing in front of her with her back to the water. I don't know if he was trying to hide her, but I could see each of them clearly. Then he pushed her over. Just gave her a little shove and she went straight down. I never heard her make a sound. The idiot just turned and started walking away as if nothing had happened. Can you believe it? He just up and pushes her over the damn rail and walks away. I didn't know what to do so I screamed. I screamed 'help' as loud as I could. I screamed out 'somebody please help that little girl. That asshole just threw that little girl over the rail.' I kept pointing and screaming. I guess he realized that I saw what he did so the son-of-a bitch started hauling ass off the pier."

"Can you describe him for me, please, Ma'am."

"Oh, five nine or five ten; skinny, at the most one forty; long, shoulder length dirty blond hair; greasy looking hair. And don't call me Ma'am!"

"I'm sorry. What was he wearing?" Detective Acer asks.

"Dark pants with a blue jean jacket . . . I think."

"Do you think that you would recognize him again?"

"You bet your badge I would! I'll probably see that creep in my head for weeks."

"That's great Ma'am. You've been an enormous help. I believe the little girl is going to be okay."

As he turns to leave she says, with a tone that clearly indicates she's frustrated with him, "Thanks for letting me know that. . . . What about the young man who saved her?"

He stops and explains, "I don't have any information on him at this time, Miss Peters."

"You're hopeless. . . . Don't you want to ask me about him? Like what he looks like, his weight, height, his age? You're not very good at what you do, are you Detective?"

"We're not looking for him. We know where he is!" he answers sharply.

"I see. . . . He's a hero you know; a real hero!" she shouts as he again turns to leave.

Abruptly turning back around, showing his own frustration, he says, "Okay, can you describe him for me?"

"Why yes; yes I can. I'm glad you asked," she mockingly says.

Waiting patiently, he says, . . . "Well!"

"He was young, nineteen, twenty, twenty-one at the most. Tall, around six one, six two, and about one eighty. He had a rather thin mustache and a short scruffy beard; you know, like one of those beards that young guys try to grow but they don't have enough yet for it to be full. He had a cap pulled down so far on his head I couldn't see his eyes but his hair hung out beneath it. It was straight, black, and long."

"You seem to remember him quite well. Why is that?" he asks.

"Because he was a hunk and I like to look at hunks! Hell, I even gave you the once-over when you first walked up."

He smiles and asks, "Have you ever seen him around here before?"

"No; just this one time. . . . It's sad isn't it, Detective? A real hero. It's so sad. It's so useless."

"Yes, Ma'am, Miss Peters. . . . Can I go now? Do you have anything else?" he says with a slight grin.

"Of course; who's stopping you."

They exchange broad smiles as he leaves.

CHAPTER FOUR

Ninety Minutes After the Incident
Saturday, March 23, 2013 at 11:30 AM

Detective Acer makes his way beneath the pier and approaches Julie Hanson, the assistant coroner. He sees her standing at the water's edge, in the shade of the pier, staring at the location where the swimmer was last seen. He takes a second to admire the statuesque figure that she possesses. Approaching slowly, not wanting to startle her, he says, "Hi Julie, do you have anything for me?"

Shaking her head, she turns and says softly, "No Steven. Not a damn thing. Nothing! . . . Several people from the pier said there was a lot of blood. Now there's nothing. It's like he never existed. No trace. We have divers in right now but are reporting nothing. It's horrible. It's just horrible."

"That it is, Baby. Are you okay? I want to hold you so much," he whispers.

"That goes for me too, my love. . . . Were you able to find anything from the clothing he threw off?" she asks hoping to hear some good news that will help in identifying this person.

"His clothing is nothing special; they appear to be brand new. No obvious hairs in the cap or anywhere. The lab will look closer but even if they do find some DNA it won't yield much of anything unless test turns up some match in the data base. I doubt that will happen giving the young age of the guy. Most of the witnesses said he was nineteen to twenty-one at the most," Steven tells her.

"No wallet? No abandoned car in the lot?" she asks.

"No, now-a-days kids that age hate to carry a wallet for some reason and all cars are accounted for."

"Did the people on the pier see what happened to him?" she asks.

"Only that he dove down just as two large sharks were approaching."

"So sad. . . . I'll see you tonight, right?" she asks knowing the answer.

"Of course, Baby. We'll drink a little white wine and watch a movie. How's that sound?" he asks.

Managing a slight smile, she says, "That's good, Honey."

CHAPTER FIVE

Eight Hours After the Incident
Saturday, March 23, 2013 at 6:00 PM

Julie approaches the front door after hearing the four soft knocks that tells her it's Steven. Bare foot and wearing a wrinkled, long sleeve, man's white dress shirt that hangs down below her shorts, she quickly unlocks the deadbolt and steps back to avoid the swing of the door. Steven pauses before entering and stares in amazement at her unpretentious beauty. Her five foot eight athletic frame is topped with short cropped jet black hair that accents her brilliant blue eyes and full pink lips.

"Well, handsome, are you going to come in or just stand there and gawk?" she says with a slight grin.

He takes a single step into the apartment, reaches out and gently caresses her chin as he lightly kisses her. He pulls back slightly, looks deep into those blue eyes while still embracing her face, and asks, "Baby, are you feeling any better?"

"Yeah, I guess I feel okay. I still can't get it out of my head though; somebody actually throwing a baby off of a pier into the Gulf of Mexico . . . and those sharks."

I've brought a couple of bottles of really good wine. At least I think it's really good because is cost six dollars a bottle compared to that three dollar stuff we usually drink. Must be twice as good," he says with a slight laugh.

"Come and sit on the couch with me," she says.

"Let me open one of these first. I also picked us up some Chinese. It's Moo Goo Gai Pan. Is that alright? I believe that's what you've ordered in the past," he says. "I just love saying that; Moo Goo Gai Pan, Moo Goo Gai Pan. I also got two extra spring rolls."

"Yes silly. Moo Goo Gai Pan is fine. And thanks Steven, for trying to cheer me up."

"It's what I do best. Here, have some of this expensive wine before we involve ourselves in that Moo," he says as he sits down beside her after she reaches out and accepts a half-full glass.

After taking a small sip, she says, "It tastes the same to me."

Steven tries it and says, "Same here; I guess I just threw my money away."

She hands the glass back to him. "I guess you did. I'm sorry. I just don't feel like wine tonight after all. I don't believe I can eat anything either. I'm sorry. I guess I'm more upset than I realized."

"I understand, Honey. Just lean back on me so that I can hold you close. It's really hard to understand how any human being can be that mean or that sick and deranged to do such a thing. But, it happens. Worst than this have occurred throughout the history of mankind; the Nazis, Stalin. Hell even here in our country we had that shooting of those little babies in Connecticut."

"Oh, Steven, why did you mention that?" she moans.

"I don't know. I guess I just wasn't thinking. I'm sorry."

"It strikes me as odd that you would think of that," she continues.

"I can see how down you are and it triggered a memory of something that happened a few days ago at the precinct. Like you, I have pretty much forgotten about Connecticut until one of the fellows at the station received an email. He forwarded it to me."

"An email; about the Connecticut killings? What did it say?"

"I'm not sure I should tell you. If I do, it's only because it puts a different viewpoint on our events relative to Connecticut and it might, in sort of a weird way, help you put today's incident in perspective."

"What is it, Steven? If it makes me forget, just for a little while what happened today, then I want to see it. I already know the details of Connecticut so it won't shock me," she explains.

"Julie, it will upset you; with the emphasis on 'will,'" Steven insists.

"Damn, Steven! Tell me! What did the email say?" she shouts.

Okay! . . . It's a fictitious account of one of the families directly involved, and their reaction."

"Oh my God! Do you have it with you?"

"Yes, I probably do. In fact I know I do. I got busy so I never got around to erasing it from my phone. . . . Julie, I'm really uneasy letting you read this," he says as he digs it out of his pocket.

Extending her hand she orders, "Hand me your phone, Steven."

"Here; it's listed under 'A Senseless Day.'"

She opens the email and begins reading:

21

A SENSELESS DAY

8:00 AM   AT WORK

CHRIS, THERE'S A PHONE CALL FOR YOU IN THE OFFICE.

CAN YOU TAKE A MESSAGE? I'M IN THE MIDDLE OF SOMETHING.

THEY SAY IT'S AN EMERGENCY AND IT'S FROM YOUR SON CHRISTOPHER'S SCHOOL.

HELLO. THIS IS CHRIS. CAN I HELP YOU?

SIR ------- I THINK YOU HAD BETTER COME TO THE SCHOOL. THERE HAS BEEN AN INCIDENT.

WHAT? WHAT KIND OF INCIDENT?

I THINK YOU SHOULD COME AS SOON AS POSSIBLE.

WHAT KIND OF INCIDENT, LADY? HE'S JUST A KINDERGARTENER. WHAT KIND OF TROUBLE CAN HE BE IN THAT WARRANTS YOU CALLING ME AT WORK?

-------- THERE HAS BEEN A SHOOTING.

OH MY GOD! IS CHRISTOPHER OKAY? DID YOU CALL NANCY, MY WIFE? NEVER MIND. I'LL CALL HER. NO ------- PERHAPS YOU SHOULD CALL HER. I'LL CALL HER!

WE COULDN'T REACH HER. WE'LL KEEP TRYING. PLEASE COME. PLEASE COME SOON.

OH MY GOD, LADY. WHAT ARE YOU SAYING?

PLEASE COME NOW.

12:00 PM   AT SCHOOL

CHRIS, NANCY; THERE IS NOTHING MORE YOU CAN DO HERE. PERHAPS YOU SHOULD GO ON HOME. YOUR

NEIGHBORS WILL ACCOMPANY YOU. THEY'RE WAITING IF YOU WANT THEM. THEY WANT TO HELP.

THANK YOU OFFICER, BUT WE ARE NOT, UNDER ANY CIRCUMSTANCES, LEAVING CHRISTOPHER HERE BY HIMSELF! ------- HE MUST BE SO COLD. HE GETS COLD SO EASILY. HE NEEDS HIS FAVORITE BLANKET; HIS SPIDERMAN BLANKET. THAT WILL WARM HIM. HE LOVES THAT BLANKET. HE TOLD ME ONCE THAT HE FEELS SAFE UNDER SPIDERMAN; THAT SPIDERMAN WILL FIGHT OFF THE BAD GUYS. CAN YOU SEE THAT HE GETS IT AND THAT HE GETS COVERED? I KNOW MY BABY'S SO COLD. HE LOVES THAT SPIDERMAN BLANKET SO.

I SURE WILL. I'LL BE HONORED TO COVER HIM. MY BOY USE TO GET COLD LIKE THAT ------- WHEN HE WAS THAT AGE. I'LL COVER HIM. I'LL TAKE CARE OF HIM.

I JUST KNOW HE'S SO COLD.

I'LL TAKE CARE OF HIM. I'LL MAKE SURE HE'S WARM.

THANK YOU.

4:00 PM   AT HOME

LOOK, HONEY, PRINCE IS WAITING FOR US AT THE WINDOW.

I KNOW. HE SITS THERE EVERY DAY. HE WAITS FOR HIM. HE JUST LOOKS OUT. HE WATCHES CHRISTOPHER GET OFF THE BUS. HE CAN'T WAIT TO SEE HIM. HE GETS SO EXCITED. LOOK AT HIS TAIL WHIP. HE'S EXPECTING TO SEE HIM.

IT'S BEEN A COUPLE OF HOURS AND PRINCE IS STILL WAITING AT THE WINDOW FOR HIM. HE DOESN'T

UNDERSTAND. ------- I DON'T UNDERSTAND. WHY'S HE STARING UP AT ME?

HE'S ASKING YOU WHERE IS HE? WHERE IS CHRISTOPHER?

PLEASE, PRINCE. STOP! STOP LOOKING AT ME! I DON'T HAVE ANY ANSWERS. OH, GOD. HE'S NOT COMING HOME. HE'S GONE! HE'S GONE! DON'T YOU UNDERSTAND? YOU STUPID DOG! STOP LOOKING AT ME FOR AN ANSWER. I DON'T HAVE AN ANSWER. NO ONE HAS ANY ANSWERS.

8:00 PM   AT HOME

I DON'T KNOW WHAT TO DO. CHRISTOPHER NEEDS HIS BATH. HE USUALLY HAS TAKEN HIS BATH BY NOW. ------- IT'S SO QUIET IN THIS HOUSE. I DON'T KNOW WHAT TO DO. TURN ON SOMETHING! IT'S TOO QUIET. PLEASE TURN ON SOME NOISE! I WANT TO TUCK HIM IN. I WANT TO TUCK HIM UNDER HIS COVERS. I WANT TO KISS HIM GOOD-NIGHT. IT'S SO QUIET. WHAT AM I GOING TO DO? WHAT ARE WE GOING TO DO? I NEED HIM HOME. HE HAS TO BE HOME. HE CAN'T STAY AT THAT SCHOOL. THAT DAMNABLE SCHOOL! ------- DID YOU FEED PRINCE?

YES, HONEY, I FED PRINCE. I TRIED TO ANYWAY. HE JUST WENT BACK TO THE FRONT WINDOW AND STARED OUT INTO THE DARK. HE'S HOPING TO SEE HIS BUDDY COME UP THE WALK.

CHRIS, WHAT ARE WE GOING TO DO? I WANT HIM HOME! DAMN! IT'S SO QUIET IN THIS DAMN HOUSE. I JUST WANT HIM HOME. HE MUST BE SO LONELY. HE'S PROBABLY WONDERING WHY HE'S ALONE; WONDERING

WHERE WE ARE; WONDERING WHEN ARE WE COMING TO PICK HIM UP. OH, GOD! I CAN'T TAKE THIS.

I KNOW, HONEY. I KNOW. I DON'T KNOW WHAT TO DO. I'M SO SCARED. I KNOW HE'S SCARED. I KNOW YOU'RE SCARED. I CAN'T HELP MY BOY. I LET HIM DOWN. I LET HIM DOWN. I SHOULD HAVE SEEN THIS COMING. I SHOULD HAVE SENSED SOMETHING.

1:00 AM   AT HOME

WHAT WAS THAT? WAS THAT HIM CRYING? I'M GOING TO CHECK ON HIM. HE NEVER CRIES OUT AT NIGHT.

IT WASN'T ANYTHING HONEY. MAYBE THE WIND. A FRONT CAME THROUGH. LIE BACK DOWN.

NO! I'M GOING TO CHECK ON HIM. MAYBE HE KICKED HIS COVERS OFF AGAIN. IT'S SO COLD TONIGHT. HE GETS SO COLD.

PLEASE, HONEY; LIE BACK DOWN.

BUT HE GETS SO COLD AND I KNOW HE'S SO LONELY. I HAVE TO HELP HIM. I HAVE TO GO TO HIM.

I KNOW, HONEY. HE HAS HIS BLANKET. THAT WILL COMFORT HIM. THAT WILL KEEP HIM WARM.

I HOPE SO. I HOPE SO. BUT I JUST WANT TO PEEP IN HIS ROOM TO SEE IF HE'S COVERED. WHY CAN'T I? HE MIGHT BE IN THERE. WHAT MAKES YOU SO SURE HE'S NOT? WHY ARE YOU BEING SO MEAN?

PLEASE, LIE BACK DOWN. TRY TO GET SOME REST. TRY TO GET SOME SLEEP.

OKAY. OKAY. ------- I GUESS HE'S WARM.

HE'S WARM HONEY. CLOSE YOUR EYES AND TRY TO REST.

7:00 AM   AT HOME
OH, GOD! I JUST WANT TO WAKE HIM UP AND GET HIM READY FOR SCHOOL. IT'S SO QUIET IN THIS DAMN HOUSE. HE IS USUALLY SO LOUD; SO BUSY AND NOISY BY THIS TIME. WHY CAN'T I GET HIM UP? WHY CAN'T HE WAKE UP? IT'S NOT FAIR. HE NEEDS TO GET READY FOR SCHOOL. THAT'S WHAT HE DOES IN THE MORNING. HE CHASES PRINCE AND PRINCE CHASES HIM. THEY MAKE SUCH A FUSS. THEY RUN SO FAST. BUT NOW, IT'S SO DAMN QUIET. I WANT TO HEAR HIM. I WANT TO SEE HIM. I WANT TO TOUCH HIM. I WANT TO HOLD HIM. I WANT TO HUG HIM AGAIN. I WANT TO YELL AT HIM TO SLOW DOWN. I DON'T UNDERSTAND. I DON'T UNDERSTAND.
I KNOW, HONEY. NO ONE DOES.
LOOK AT THE SKY THIS MORNING CHRIS. LOOK AT HOW LONELY IT LOOKS. IT'S SUCH A LONELY LOOKING SKY. WHY WOULD GOD MAKE SUCH A LONELY LOOKING DAY; A DAY WITH NOTHING; A DAY SO LONESOME? WHY? I JUST WANT ONE GOOD HAPPY DAY. I JUST WANT ONE MORE DAY WITH OUR SON. IS THAT TOO MUCH TO ASK? JUST ONE DAY; NOT THIS DAMNABLE LONELY DAY BUT A CHEERFUL DAY TO SPEND WITH CHRISTOPHER. ------- A DAY TO SAY GOOD BYE.
NO, I DON'T THINK THAT IS TOO MUCH TO ASK AT ALL.
------- OH MY GOD! I WANT OUR LITTLE BOY HOME!

Julie wipes away tears as Steven says, "I'm sorry, Baby. I shouldn't have let you read it."

"I'm okay, Steven. . . . Take me to bed. Please take me to bed and make love to me."

CHAPTER SIX

Twenty-Two Hours After the Incident
Sunday, March 24, 2013 at 8:00 AM

Entering the precinct the next morning, a smiling Detective Acer says, "It looks like the local TV channels really helped in catching the SOB. Congrats to all involved."

"Where were you? We tried calling but it seems that your phone was shut down," states a fellow officer.

"I had to put out a personal fire."

"Is Julie okay now, Detective Acer?" he asks with a grin.

"She's fine. Thanks for asking. I'm glad you're so concerned. Now, somebody bring me up to speed."

"The manager of Daisy's helped by responding to a request by the TV channels to report to the police any suspicious actions or activities at, or immediately following the time of the incident. He described a guy who came into his place and created a scene about ten minutes after the time. His description matched those of the witnesses on the pier. He was also able to give us a description of his car. He said one of his customers saw a Florida license. He didn't get the number. But, that little girl knowing her name was the key. We contacted several James households in the local areas, in and around Pensacola. We were able to locate Margaret James, the mother of Abigail James, better known as Abby, living in Pensacola Beach. Officers were at the house when this Einstein asshole drove right up without noticing anything, apparently because he was as high as a kite. The idiot actually parked in the drive. That was it. He didn't resist."

"What is the suspect's name and what did he have to say?" Detective Acer asks.

"His name is Justin Webb; sort of a serial trouble maker but no major arrests or convictions. The arresting officer reported that Mr. Webb was shocked to see them, but all he would say was that Ms. James, Abby's mother, put him up to it. That it was her plan. That she wanted to get rid of Abby in order to be able to spend more time with him," the officer says with a grin.

"He actually blamed the mother? What was her reaction?"

"She was distraught. She just held onto Abby; wouldn't let anyone near her. She wouldn't let her out of her sight the entire time we were there at the house." the officer explains.

"I see. What sort of comments did Ms. James give?"

"She screamed over and over that Webb's crazy. That's she's been trying to get him out of her house. She was growing more and more concerned about his bizarre actions even though he had recently started a new job."

Detective Acer holds up his cup of coffee in a toast and announces, "Well, thanks again fellows; and you gals too. Y'all did a great job. I want to be at that trial when Mr. Webb explains his defense. I can see it now, 'Ladies and Gentlemen of the Jury, I threw a beautiful five year old little girl off a twenty foot high fishing pier into the cold waters of the shark infested Gulf of Mexico because her mother wanted me, not her.' What a joke."

+ + + +

Four months later Mr. Justin Webb was found guilty and sentenced to twenty-five years in the state penitentiary without the benefit of parole.

PART TWO

Before The Incident

CHAPTER SEVEN

6 Months Before The Incident
Thursday, September 13, 2012 at 5:00 PM

Margaret James's shift at Peggy's Beauty Salon is finally over. She glances quickly into her station's mirror and decides to run a brush through her shoulder length blond hair. She tells herself. . . I'm far above average looking but should do something with that hair color because it doesn't suit me very well; with my dark eyebrows, deep brown eyes, and olive skin. I'm twenty-three and should have a more natural look.

"Bye, everyone! See y'all tomorrow," she shouts as she leaves the salon.

"Bye, Maggie!"

She's eager to get off her feet; to rush home to her lovable little four and half year old Abigail. It's a blessing that Abby's at home and that she doesn't have to go pick her up at that expensive and depressing daycare center. However, it's not clear to her if it's a good idea or not, that Justin Webb, her recently unemployed, live-in boyfriend, is the one keeping her during the day. Lately he can be a little trying.

+ + + +

"Justin, where's Abby?" Margaret asks as she enters the living room and glances around the rather small area.

"I think she's in the back room," Justin mumbles without making any effort to get off the couch. "You might want to check the kitchen too."

"You think?" she shouts. "You're not sure where she is?"

"I told you where to look! Are you hard of hearing?" he returns the shout.

Margaret finds her sitting next to the refrigerator with her knees drawn to her chest and caressing her favorite stuffed teddy bear. She asks her, "Abby baby, what are you doing?"

"I couldn't open the door," she pitifully answers.

Margaret picks her up and carries her back to the living room as she yells at Justin, "Get your lazy skinny ass off of my couch and go get a gallon of milk at the Quick Stop! When did Abby last eat?"

"I found a couple of cans of tuna in the damn pantry. We had some around noon. She didn't eat much. I figured she wasn't hungry," he answers as he slowly stands.

"Have you been drinking?" she yells.

"I had two beers at lunch with the tuna fish and another an hour ago. So what?" he defiantly shouts.

"Get the hell out of here! Go get me the milk, come back, pack up your things, and leave!" she demands still caressing Abby.

"I'll go get the milk but my ass is not going anywhere else!" he boldly states.

"Get out!"

"I'll be back in ten minutes!"

"Bring back a jar of peanut butter and a loaf of bread too," she demands but with a lower voice.

He senses that she is backing down ever so slightly. He smiles within himself because he feels that he has won this round. "Give me more money! How am I going to buy all that shit? I ain't got enough," he orders with confidence.

+ + + +

"Hey, Mahatma! Where you keep the damn milk? I want the whole milk kind, not that watery skim stuff," Justin shouts as he enters the Quick Stop.

"I'm sorry, Sir. You must have me confused with someone else. My name is not Mahatma!" the clerk politely says. "But Sir, you can find the milk in the coolers against the back wall."

"All you brown folks from India look alike to me Mahatma. It's fresh, right; the milk that is? And Mahatma, didn't you invent some kind of special rice or something? Seems like I've heard that somewhere," Justin continues.

"If you want rice it's on the bottom shelf, on the aisle to the right," the clerk again politely responds.

Looking around the store, Justin bellows, "Come on Mahatma; now where did you hide the damn bread? I can't find a single loaf anywhere. You should try to organize this disgusting mess. Look, you have a goddamn jar of dill pickles next to a two pound bag of sugar. Do you know anyone who puts sugar on pickles? I sure don't."

"As I have previously mentioned Sir, my name is not Mahatma! The bread is up here by the checkout counter!" he says while attempting to maintain his self control but having a tough time of it.

"Okay, Mahatma, I'll just call you India."

"Fine, whatever you say. Just get what you need and please go! Pay me and get out of my store!"

"You kicking me out, India? You have some goddamn nerve talking to me like that. I'm the customer. I can do no wrong. This is America. The customer is always right in America! Who's your boss? You must report to someone. What's his name? Is it Ganhdi? You have some nerve," Justine rants on as he sees the clerk turn away for a split second. It's just enough time for him to slip a jar of peanut butter under his waist band and cover it with his tee shirt.

While checking out, the clerk spots the jar and punches the police call button under the counter. Before Justin reaches half way to his car a Police cruiser pulls up with its lights flashing and siren blaring. Justin hits his knees and begins crying, "Please Mr. Officer, don't arrest me! I lost my job. I don't have much money for food. I was just hungry. Please don't arrest me. Here it is, take it! Or I'll pay for it. I have a couple of bucks. Please!" he begs.

Remaining on his knees, Justin watches as the officer approaches the clerk. He suspects that they are discussing the situation. The officer returns and orders sternly, "Get off your knees and return the peanut butter to the gentleman."

Justin walks over to the clerk, sarcastically flips the jar to him, and says, "Thanks for nothing, India."

The officer grabs him by the arm and shoves him in the direction of his car while shouting, "You worthless skinny piece of crap! I should arrest you even if he didn't want to press charges. Get the hell out of my sight!"

"Yes, Sir, Sir! I won't be no more problem," he says as he jumps in his car and drives off with a victorious smile.

CHAPTER EIGHT

Six Months Before the Incident
Thursday, September 13, 2012 at 6:45 PM

"Maggie!" Justin excitedly yells out as he returns to the apartment. "Guess the hell what? I nearly got my ass arrested."

"Arrested? I wondered why you were taking so long. What'd you do now?" she asks from the kitchen. "And keep your voice down. Abby just went down?"

"Oh, this idiot Indian dude at the store said I was stealing peanut butter. Not a Tonto type Indian but one of those Dodge My Ball types."

Returning to the living room, carrying two beers and a plate of saltines and Swiss cheese, she asks, after hiding a grin but still with a confused expression, "What the hell are you talking about Justin? Why did he say you were stealing? And I believe you mean Taj Mahal."

"Whatever. It was probably because he spotted the jar under this damn shirt?" he answers as he gives it a quick tug.

"You tried to hide a jar of peanut butter under that skin tight tee shirt you're wearing?" She pauses a second then continues, "You wanted to get caught, didn't you?"

"Well, I've been cooped up in here all damn day with your kid and I wanted a little excitement," he explains.

"By getting arrested?"

"I've almost been arrested before. It's no big deal," he argues.

"I know! You pulled this same type of stunt a couple of months ago at your job. I believe you got into it with your foreman over how many bricks you laid when all he had to do was stand there and count the ones on the wall you put up."

"Well, I was bored then too. A little argument with the boss would be exciting. If I got fired that would be a bonus; I'd get to spend more time with you," he says with an aren't-you-lucky grin.

"These types of actions are going to get us in trouble," she states with a matter-of-fact tone.

"I can control myself. Don't you worry your pretty little ass. As long as me and you are together, nothing can happen. You make me happy. I love you. Me and you forever!" he exclaims with confidence.

She takes notice that he never mentioned Abby.

"You're sweet, but I think, in fact I know, that it's more than that. It's more than you wanting excitement. It's about you wanting to get caught. Instead of you going about your own business in a normal civilized way; instead of you blending in at the store or at a job, you stand out on purpose," Maggie explains. "You can be excited about things and not stand out. You do realize that, right Justin?"

"That's ridiculous, My Sweet. Where'd you get that line of bull crap? I just like a little innocent trouble making. Why the hell would I want to get caught?" he asks as he gives her a longing, come to me look.

"You are probably not doing it consciously but subconsciously you definitely want to get caught! . . . Don't look at me like that. Turn those sexy eyes of yours away," she says with a wide grin that is hiding an uncertainty, a fear that his quest for a thrill will continue and eventually lead to riskier actions.

He giggles, grabs the two beers, and motions for her to follow him to the bedroom.

She's continues with her train-of-thought as she unhurriedly reaches for the saltines and cheese . . . "Four months ago when I met Justin he was a sweet and caring guy. A fun, reckless, devil-may-care, never could keep his mouth shut guy. But, he was cute, a good lover, and an overall blast to be around. Plus, he seemed to enjoy being around Abby and she around him. That was until he lost that job. He never was going to be a brain surgeon but he did bring in a paycheck and he was nice to me and Abby. He's changed. Now I'm not so sure I can trust him. Do I put up with his reckless antics much longer or tell him he has to go before something else happens? There's a distinct possibility that someone is going to get hurt; him, me, or my sweet Abby. I can't have that."

She practices that smile again while slowly joining him in the bedroom.

CHAPTER NINE

Six Months Before the Incident
Friday, September 14, 2012 at 7:30 AM

The next morning, as Margaret was walking out of the door to go to the salon, Justin shouts from the bedroom, "Maggie, I'm so sorry about my actions yesterday. I'm sorry I didn't keep a better eye on Abby and I'm sorry about that stupid episode with the store clerk. . . . Please know that I will never let anything happen to Abby. . . . Maggie, did you hear me?"

"Yes, Justin. Thanks for saying that. It means a lot to me," she answers as she pauses at the door.

"Then you forgive me?" he asks as he approaches her.

"Yes, Justin. I forgive you."

"Great!" he exclaims. "And guess what?"

"What, Justin? I have to go or I will be late."

"I'm going to take Abby to the playground. She loves those stupid swings and that big ass slide. There's always a bunch of other little idiot kids around who she likes to play with," he enthusiastically announces.

"That's a good idea. Make sure you behave yourself. Y'all have fun. I have to go," she says as she rushes to her car.

Arriving at the playground, Justin says, "Okay Abby. Here we are. Go, girl, go! Have fun. I'll be sitting right over there on that bench if you need me."

I won't need you. I'm big now," she says.

"Yes you are. Just the same, I'll be right there. First I'm going to run across the street to that little store and get me some smokes and something to drink. I'll just be a second. What do you want, chocolate milk or orange juice?"

"Chocolate milk," she yells as she heads for the slide.

Returning, he sees Abby playing on the swings; trying to push herself but not having much luck. Justin calls out to her, "Abby, I thought that you were going to play on the slide."

She runs up to him and says as she points, "I wanted to but that mean big boy over there wouldn't let me. He kept blocking the ladder. He said he's six and can do what he wants."

"Really! Well, if you want to go down the slide you go right ahead. I'll make sure that brat won't stop you," he says as he stares at the boy who is now playing on the marry-go-round.

"Okay."

She runs toward the slide. The boy on the merry-go-round jumps off and also rushes to the slide. He jumps and stands at the foot of the ladder, blocking Abby as she approaches. Justin sees what has happens and walks over. He calmly says, "Excuse me little boy. This little girl wants to use the slide. It's for everybody. Can you please step aside?"

"No!" the boys shouts. "I don't want her to!"

"It's not up to you, Sonny. So get the hell out of the way!" a startled Justin orders.

"No!"

Justin has seen enough. He reaches down and grabs the boy by his upper arms and lifts him without saying a word. He places him down a few feet to the side of the ladder as Abby scurries up to the top.

The boy screams out at the top of his lungs, "Help! This man grabbed me! Help me! Mama, help!"

Out of the corner of his eye, Justin sees a woman running toward them.

Breathless after her short jaunt, the obviously overweight mother yells, "Get away from my little boy! Leave him along!"

Justin backs away as Abby makes her first trip down the slide.

He says, "I just moved the brat aside. He wouldn't let my little girl go down the damn slide. Why isn't he in school? Did he flunk out of kindergarten?"

"I'm calling the police! How dare you put your filthy hands on my little boy! Little girl, has he hurt you?" she asks Abby as she searches in her purse apparently for a cell phone.

"No," Abby answers as she makes another trip up the ladder.

"Lady, are you crazy? No one has hurt these kids; except maybe your big mouth. Please don't call the police. I'm begging your fat ass."

"I just did. I pressed 911. They'll track my phone and will be here in a minute," she informs him.

"You dumb bitch. Do you have any idea what you have done?" Abby, hurry down! We have to go! We have to go now!"

They all hear the police sirens approaching.

"That's your behind now; you child molester!" the woman snarls.

+ + + +

Abby was taken by child services and held until Margaret arrived. She was released into her custody later that evening.

Justin was hand cuffed, thrown into the back of the police cruiser, taken down to central lockup, and booked with child molestation pending further investigation. A week later, after the police interviewed several witnesses to the incident, Justin was released with only a warning.

"Maggie! Did you hear the good news? All those goddamn charges have been dropped! I'm a free man. I don't have to worry about jail! . . . Maggie, did you hear me. Did you hear what I said?" he shouts with glee.

"I heard! . . . I want you out of my house. I want you to leave tomorrow morning. Do you hear me? Did you hear what I said?" she mocks him. Margaret knew before saying this that it would take more than a simple demand to get him to leave. She'll need a plan; one that will appear to him to be in his own best interest before he would ever consider leaving.

With his merriment quickly turning to misery, he sternly states, "As I've told you before, My Sweet. My ass is not going anywhere. It will always be with you and yours will always be with me. The quicker your pea brain realizes that, the quicker we can get along with our lives together."

CHAPTER TEN

Three Months Before The Incident
Thursday, December 6, 2012 at 6:30 PM

"Justin, I think we should move from Gulf Shores. I'm sick and tired of my job and all its internal politics," Margaret announces one evening after returning from work.

"That's fine with me. Just say the word and I'll start packing our crap."

"I need a change. I want to move to Pensacola Beach and get a part-time job styling hair. Part-time because I want to go back to school on a full time basis and get a teaching degree. I have a little savings and with a student loan I can afford it. I figure if I double up on some of the courses and take daytime as well as night classes I can graduate in about a year and a half. I have several of my basis courses out of the way from when I went before, right after high school. The University of West Florida has an excellent teaching curriculum. I want to teach little kids; first through third grade. It might take a huge effort from each of us but that's okay, I know we can do it. What do you think?"

"Damn, Maggie; that's a great idea! I bet I could easily get a goddamn job there; it being such a big area, with many more people and businesses than around here," he says excitedly.

"That right. You've been behaving yourself lately so you should be able to get something with your new attitude and you'll have much better luck keeping it. Plus, as an added bonus, we will be bringing in more money so I will be able to enroll Abby in a quality daycare center," she says. "We wouldn't have to fool with her a good part of the day."

"Let's do it Maggie!" he exclaims.

"Consider it done. I'll give my notice tomorrow at work and you can start the packing. I want to enroll in UWF this month. Their spring semester starts next month; the first part of January."

"Let's open that stupid box of red wine we've been saving and celebrate," he suggests.

"Great! Let me get Abby down and out of our hair then we will be able to do more than drink wine," she says with a teasing smile.

He answers by saying, "You are my kind of mama!"

CHAPTER ELEVEN

Two Months Before The Incident
Monday, January 14, 2013 at 7:00 AM

"Justin, I just love our new place here in Pensacola Beach and the fact that I'm a student again. . . .You do remember that after work I go to my first class this afternoon? I have three today. The first one is at one o'clock and the last one is a night class," Maggie calls out from the bathroom as she gets geared up for the day. "Did you get Abby ready to go? I'll drop her off at the preschool."

"Right. Sounds like you will have a lot of time in between. What time do you think you'll be home?" he asks from the kitchen.

"I imagine not until around nine. I'll just hang out around campus and work on any assignments I might have. I've heard that they have a great indoor swimming pool. I'm going to check it out. I've been thinking I might bring my suit and swim. I could surely use the exercise. . . . Don't forget to pick her up after you get off work," she says.

"I won't and yes she's ready," he answers. "The pool sounds great."

She takes Abby by the hand and hurriedly runs out the door. Stopping, she looks back and throws a kiss to Justin. "I'll see you tonight. Take good care of this little girl until I get home."

Abby looks up at her and smiles. Justin doesn't comment nor smile.

CHAPTER TWELVE

Two Months Before The Incident
Wednesday, January 23, 2013 at 4:00 PM

"Hi, my name is Richard Rubio. Would you mind if I joined you? It seems all the tables are occupied. For the number of students at this university this library is way too small. It needs to be about twice the size."

"No. Please do. There's lot of room here," Maggie answers glancing at him and then quickly around the study room.

"Thanks," he says as he finds himself unable to look away from her face and eyes. . . . "I won't be in your way. . . . I'll just spread out down on this end." He indicates where he will locate as he's finally able to break his enchantment by looking down and pulling out a chair.

"No problem. I'm Margaret James."

"Are you a student here at UWF, Margaret James? I mean, I know that you're a student. That is, I think you are since you're here in the school library and have your books and papers spread all over. . . . I'm sorry, it's none of my business. I'll shut up and sit down over here. Over there where I pointed earlier," he says clumsily.

"Yes, I'm a student. . . . She looks at him and asks, "Can you answer a question for me?"

"Sure," he says as he finally takes his seat. "I'll try to answer. That is, if I know the answer. If I don't, I'll tell you I don't know. . . . Oh, God! . . . What is the question? Please hurry and ask it before I lose consciousness."

She chuckles and says, "Actually, I now have two questions."

"Oh, good grief!"

"First, are you majoring in public speaking? If you are, you should consider changing. And secondly, why did you pick this table? I looked around and there are at least a half dozen others that you could have chosen."

He pauses and again looks intently at her and says, . . . "No, I'm a physical education major. I'm just having a little trouble right now doing two things at once; getting my words to come out in the correct order and look at you. As far as to why I picked this particular table, it was because it seemed to be the most interesting table available."

"What did you find so interesting about it?" she continues with an ever so slight grin.

"Well first, I noticed that the table top is quite flat and has a really nice shine. I like shiny things, especially shiny fake wood. Then I saw that the chairs appeared to be more comfortable than those at the other tables. My tail bone starts to ache after sitting in uncomfortable chairs for an extended period," he facetiously answers.

"I can understand that."

"Really?" he says not taking his eyes off of her.

"Yes. I also like shiny things."

"And your tail bone?" he probes.

"Now don't you worry your cute little self about my tail bone," she says with a broader grin.

". . . . Now it's my turn, Margaret James. Why did you agree to let me join you?"

"Because I felt sorry for you," she quickly answers.

"Sorry for me? What made you feel sorry for me?"

"You just stood there with your mouth wide open. I didn't want you to humiliate yourself by drooling all over this shiny table top; therefore, I said you could sit here."

"Was I that obvious?" he asks.

"Oh, yes; yes you were, Richard Rubio."

"Please call me Rick."

"Hello Rick. You can call me Maggie."

After nearly thirty minutes of practically complete silence as they each pretend to be concentrating on their studies, Maggie says, "I've got a class in about an hour. I want to get some nourishment beforehand. Would you like to join me over a hot dog? Amazingly, they're pretty tasty at the Union. Dutch treat."

"I'd love to!" Rick excitedly says. "But I'm buying."

CHAPTER THIRTEEN

Two Months Before the Incident

Wednesday, *January 23, 2013 at 4:45 PM*

They locate a scarce vacant table near a large picture window that looks out over one of the student parking lots. She tosses her book bag on one of the chairs and says, "Since you're picking up the tab I'll go get the goodies. Keep an eye on my stuff."

"I like mine smothered in chili and melted cheddar cheese," he says.

"I thought that you were a phys ed major. Aren't you guys into eating, quote unquote, correctly?"

"Okay, tell them not to melt the cheese."

Finishing their brief meal, Rick asks, as he watches her closely, "Do you live close by the school, Maggie James?"

"No, I actually have a place on Pensacola Beach."

"Do you live alone?"

"If you're asking if I'm married; no I'm not and never have been. I live with a guy. His name is Justin."

"I see." he says.

Seeing the disappointment in his body language, she says, "Don't be too concerned about him. However, I should also mention that I do have a beautiful little girl that's almost five. Her name is Abby."

"Is Justin her father?"

"No, that bum split about six weeks after she was born. Haven't seen hide nor hair of his worthless ass since. What about you?"

"I live in Navarre. That's about twenty miles east of Pensacola Beach. I work at a dive shop there. We give diving lessons, scuba and snorkeling. We also offer diving trips to offshore sights; to sunken old boats and ships. The navy sunk a world war two aircraft carrier, the Oriskany, in two hundred feet of water about six years ago just about twenty miles offshore. It's a great place to take serious divers."

"Is that right? You seem to really be into diving. Do you actually lead these types of tour? Do you dive yourself?" she asks with a true tone of interest.

"Oh, yeah! I love it," he exclaims. "I'm been swimming since I was two, dove off high diving boards around seven, and started scuba diving at fifteen. I did year-round competitive swimming and platform diving through high school. In short, I'm part fish," he laughs.

She smiles as she studies him.

"My ideal goal in my life is to own my own shop; plus a dive boat. I like to design underwater apparatuses to help the average weekend diver stay under longer and move faster through the water. I'm saving up to get my shop and get enough money to prove my designs."

"Where do you do the actually teaching of a beginner?" she asks with a growing interest.

"We have a small pool at the shop where we teach the basics then we gradually move to offshore waters."

"I've been thinking about doing some swimming here, in UWF's pool. I went by it the other day. It's fantastic. They even have diving boards. I'd love to learn how to dive. I'm a poor swimmer but I would like to improve. I need lessons," she proclaims, hoping that he will pick up on the hint and offer to teach her.

"Why don't you let me give you a few lessons? Since we're students we can use the pool. January is our slowest time at the shop."

She's thinking . . . he bit; hook, line, and sinker. "Fantastic!"

"That's great! The day after tomorrow, I'll meet you at the pool after your class. A little after six, right?"

"That'll work," she answers as she grabs her backpack, looks at him with a broad smiles, and winks.

CHAPTER FOURTEEN

Two Months Before the Incident
Friday, January 25, 2013 at 6:20 PM

Maggie dangles her feet in the water as she sits at the pool's edge. She stares at Rick as he approaches from the men's locker room. "Hi Rick. I'm ready for my lessons?" she says while not being able to take her eyes off of his shirtless body. That jet black shaggy hair, mustache, and his scruffy beard only serves to accent his hairless swimmer's chest and six pack abdomen.

"Hello, Maggie. You look quite stunning this evening," he says as he notices her watching him.

"You look pretty impressive yourself," she counters.

He laughs and says, "Shall we get started?"

"Great! I'm ready."

"Now, what is it that you would like to work on? What stroke; the freestyle, back, or perhaps the breast stroke? I would think that you would be pretty good at the breast stroke," he adds with a grin.

"Now, what makes you say that?" she asks as she lifts herself with her arms and slides into the cool water. "Wow, that's pretty chilly!"

"It will feel better as soon as we get moving," he shouts out as he dives in, circles around underwater, and startles her as he springs up from behind.

"Ah! You scared me!"

He grabs her shoulders, tilts her back, and while supporting her head, says, "Swing your arms over your head like a windmill and kick your feet."

He smiles as she does a perfect backstroke, rolls over onto her stomach, swims freestyle completely across the pool, performs a perfect flip turn, and returns. Still smiling and admiring her form, he says, "Somebody has been putting me on. You're a damn good swimmer."

"You caught me," she says with a laugh. "What I really would like to learn is how to go off the high diving board; jump off, not dive."

"I see. Well that's a snap. It's literally like falling off a log if all you want to do is jump."

"I've tried it before but I get petrified," she explains.

"What scares you?"

"Water going up my nose; I jumped once and saw stars because of all the water rushing up my nostrils and into my brain," she clarifies with a serious tone.

"No problem. Let's go climb up the ladder. I'll be right behind you."

The board bends as she walks slowly out to within two feet of the end. As it slowly bounces she nervously asks, "Now what?"

He steps on the board causing it to bend further. The bouncing continues as he walks slowly up behind her. She screams as he yells into her ear, "Hold your nose!" and pushes her off the end. He follows her in with a beautiful jackknife dive.

Coming up spiting water she manages to finally say, "You're some instructor!"

"You did great, but practice makes perfect! Are you ready to go again?" he asks.

"That's okay. There's no need. I'm a fast learner."

His hardy laughter subsides as he says, "You are beautiful. Would you mind if I kiss you?"

"Thank you, and no," she softly says with a smile. Then she yells, "But you have to catch me first!"

She takes off heading toward the shallower end of the pool. He laughs and watches her swim a short distance before starting his pursuit. He catches her but not before she reaches the wall.

"I win!" she shouts wiping the water from her eyes and face.

"Oh, yeah! I don't care," he says as he whips his head from side to side, shaking the water from his long hair. He smiles as he bends forward and kisses her gently.

The touch of his mustache and the taste of the chlorine treated water ignite her senses. She can feel that he too shares her exhilaration. He caresses her face and kisses her long and hard this time. She playfully pulls away and dives underwater and attempts to swim away. He dives after her, follows, and grabs her ankles pulling her back and beneath him. He grads her around her shoulders as they spring to the surface. They kiss again as they fall back under the water. They hold their caress as they settle to the bottom.

Surfacing with broad smiles, they hear someone shout out, "Hey you two! Take the love making out of my pool and someplace else! There's a motel down the street that rents by the hour! . . . Now get the hell out of the pool!"

"Okay, okay! We're leaving," they shout with a giggle as they climb out and run to the dressing rooms.

"And no running on the pool deck!" he bellows as he turns to continue his patrol.

CHAPTER FIFTEEN

Two Months Before the Incident
Friday, January 25, 2013 at 9:30 PM

"I'm home! . . . Justin!" Maggie calls out as she enters.

"I'm in here with Abby. She just now closed her goddamn eyes. I'm been trying to get her little ass asleep for over an hour. So stop the damn yelling, already!" he shouts in a whispering frustrated voice.

Peaking into Abby's bedroom, she asks, "Why is she still up? It's nearly nine thirty."

"Because we didn't get home until late," he says as they each move into the living room.

"Why? You can pick her up any time after your work. I thought that you got off at four?"

"Right, I do, but I had to run a little errand first. I got there a little after six. Some old biddy wouldn't release her to me. Said I wasn't authorized are some such crap," he attempts to explain.

"That's the night lady! I gave the note that I wrote allowing you to pick Abby up to her daytime teacher. This night lady probably didn't know anything about it." Sensing something went awry, Maggie continues and asks, "You didn't get into to some sort of confrontation at Abby's daycare, did you Justin?"

"Well, it didn't start out as a confrontation. I was very polite."

"Damnit, Justin; what happened?" she screams while trying to hold her voice down in order not to awaken Abby.

"The old bat kept telling me that I had to leave. That I couldn't hang around. I told her I wasn't going anywhere without Abby," he sheepishly answers.

"Continue, Justin," Maggie manages to calmly say.

"Well. The bitch up and calls the cops. By the time I got it all settled out with them and those goddamn child services assholes, it was after eight o'clock when we got home."

Gradually collecting her thoughts she asks, "What sort of errand did you have to run that was so important that you would leave Abby at that school?"

Justin casually answers, "I had to replenish my stash. I was down to my last joint."

"You've been smoking weed?" she hollers. "Around Abby?"

"I told you already that if you keep screaming she is going to wake up. So stop! And yes, I smoke weed; and I do it around your kid. I have been for months. I have to; it calms my nerves."

Maggie turns around and stands without a comment. Then thinking, as she walks into the kitchen . . . that was the last straw. I've got to get this guy out of my house. I'll start putting my plan into action. I realize, up until tonight, that the plan was more wishful thinking than anything. But after tonight, with drugs now coming into the picture, it has to be for real. Being with Richard Rubio at the pool tonight convinces me that it was workable. I'll start now; tonight.

+ + + +

Justin follows her into the kitchen and asks, "Why are you so quiet? Don't you want to yell at me?"

"No, Baby. There's no need to yell at you. You are you. I should realize that by now. You're going to get into some kind of crazy trouble because it's you. That's what you do. Actually I think it's kind of funny. My life would be such a bore without you in it. However, I wish that Abby wasn't involved so much. If someone would look at our situation from afar they would say, that in the last couple of instances, she is the problem. Don't you agree that it would seem that way to some outsider?"

"I guess so," he says confused as he just stares at her.

She continues, "Can I fix you something; a bowl of cereal, ice cream, anything? I grabbed a burger on the way home."

"No, My Sweet; I'm just going to have one of those damn beers that I saw in the back of the frig."

"Well don't sip on it too long. I want some serious loving from you tonight. For some reason I'm feeling really horny," she says with a broad smile as she nods her head toward the bedroom.

"Oh, yeah? Horny? You said horny?"

"Yes, my skinny little hunk. That's the word; horny. I'm horny!"

"Oh, my!" he utters.

Just above a whisper she says, "But, first I'm going to take a shower. Why don't you join me? I need to get this smelly chlorine out of my hair. If you'll wash mine I'll wash yours."

"What? . . . We, we've never done that before," he says with a stammer as he hurriedly downs the beer and energetically bangs the empty can on the metal kitchen table.

"It's just me, you, and a bar of soft soap tonight. No one else," she says.

"Oh, my!" he exclaims as he kicks off his shoes into a corner, hops on alternate feet as he removes his socks and flips them over his shoulder, pulls his tee shirt over his head and tosses it toward the table, steps out of his pants and boxers and leaves them in a ball on the floor, and runs naked from the kitchen swinging his arms over his head as he yells, "Here comes your hunk!"

She laughs hardily at the sight of him running towards her. Grabbing her, he says, "Just the two of us!"

At that exact instance, Abby cries out from her room, "Mommy, what's all the noise? I'm scared. Can you come and sleep with me?"

Justin's head drops and his shoulders stoop as his once soaring spirit and consequent anatomy plummet.

CHAPTER SIXTEEN

Five Weeks Before The Incident
Friday, February 1, 2013 at 6:15 PM

Rick finds Maggie at her usual spot; dangling her feet in the cool water at the edge of the pool. She looks up at him and says, "Hello, handsome."

"Hi, beautiful. You look so lovely sitting there like that."

"Thank you."

"But, I'm afraid that you're going to have to give me a rain check for tonight's swim," he says as he approaches.

"Oh, yeah. I'll have you know young man, I'm not use to getting stood up," she jokes. "What's going on?"

"My boss called me this morning and wants me to take the boat and get it ready for the spring break crowd. That means that I have to take it out in the morning and go clean the bottom," he explains.

"What does that have to do with tonight?" she asks as she gets to her feet and gives him a quick kiss.

"The boat hasn't been run for quite a while and I should go and check things out tonight. That way all I'll have to do is jump in it tomorrow morning and be off." He pauses a moment then excitedly continues, "You know what? Why don't you come with me tomorrow morning? It's a huge boat!"

"What am I going to do on some yucky old huge boat? I don't fish."

He smiles as he imagines the possibilities.

"What are you grinning about?" she asks with a grin of her own.

"Let me tell you about this old yucky boat! It's about thirty feet long and ten feet wide. In addition to all the diving gear on the deck, it has a cabin. In the cabin, and here's where it get exciting, there's a stove, a microwave, a sink, a bathroom with a shower, a frig, and a table!" he exclaims.

"Whoopty-doo! What is it that you want; whip you up some lunch?"

"Nope. . . . On second thought, maybe you could bring a few sandwiches and some chips because I'm going to bring two bottles of merlot."

Still with that slight grin that gives away her thought that he's up to something, she asks, "Rick, what the hell are you talking about?"

"A sleeping berth! . . . A bed! . . . A bed that's never been used!" he shouts with elation as he picks her up and swings her around.

"Are you telling me that you are going to get me on your old yucky boat to bed me?" she asks again with that grin.

"No, I'm saying that I am going to get you on that old boat to screw you."

"Oh! In that case I'll see you in the morning."

CHAPTER SEVENTEEN

Seven Weeks Before The Incident
Saturday, February 2, 2013 at 11:00 PM

Following his precise directions, Maggie pulls up to the covered boat slip that's located behind the dive shop. She steps out of her car, pauses, and stares in amazement. Due to her limited maritime experience, she can only identify what she's looking at as a cabin cruiser. It has a like-new bright white deck that is partially surrounded by a shiny chrome handrail. The aft or rear section is a large open area with closed compartments that she presumes holds the stowed away diving equipment. The cabin has three circular operational portholes on each side. Above the cabin sits a glass enclosed pilot house. All of this is supported by a glossy midnight blue hull.

She calls out, "Rick I'm here! Just as I suspected, an old yucky boat! . . . What do you want me to do?"

Emerging from the cabin he answers, "Well for starters, you might want to come aboard this old tub."

"You want me to step across this gap?" she asks as she points at the space between the boat and the dock.

"It's only about eighteen inches, for heaven's sake. You're a real dare devil aren't you?" he asks giggling as he extends his hand.

"I think so," she answers as she grabs it, balances, and takes a quick step onto the deck. The boat rolls slightly but due to its size it's barely noticeable.

"Did you bring the sandwiches and chips?" he asks as he gives her a hello kiss on the cheek.

"I did. . . . Is that the only greeting I get for coming all this way and then risking my limbs by climbing on to this thing? 'Did you bring the food?' What a welcome."

In silence he gently grabs and tilts her head back as he looks into her face. He lightly kisses her forehead before moving down to her eyes, kissing softly the right and then the left. Then he teasingly pecks all around her mouth. Pulling slightly back, he asks, "Is that better?"

"Better, but not perfect." She can't take it any longer so she reaches up and pulls his head down and gives him a hard and long kiss.

"Now that's the way you properly greet someone! Let me demonstrate again so you don't forget," she says with vigor as she grabs behind his head.

"Whoa. We have to slow down. I have to clean the bottom of this tub, remember?"

"You were serious? You really have to work?" she asks. "How are you going to do that? We're floating!"

"I'm going to take her out to Back Bay and anchor in four to five feet of water. Then I'm going to get my little brush, scraper, and mask and jump overboard. After that I'm going to dive under and proceed to scrape and brush off the bad old barnacles and marine growth from the bottom of this tub."

"It's February; the water is freezing. It won't be very long before you start turning blue," she says with some concern, but not much.

"I won't be in that long. I estimate thirty to forty-five minutes based on what I can see from up here. Plus, I'll wear a wetsuit. It keeps me pretty warm."

"Wetsuit? Is that the skin tight black thing that covers you from head to toe?" she asks. "I bet you will look great in it; with those long legs."

"I look a lot better out of it," he says with a grin. "Can you fix me one of those sandwiches while I slip into the suit? I want to eat something before I go; gives me a little energy."

"Gladly, you're going to need it," she says smiling.

CHAPTER EIGHTEEN

Seven Weeks Before The Incident
Saturday, February 2, 2013 at 12:30 PM

She watches him in silence as he climbs back aboard after completing his task. He doesn't notice her standing on the lowest step of the open entryway to the cabin. He stands tall in the center of the open deck and stretches his arms that apparently were fatigued from the cleaning. He removes his cap, tosses it into a corner, and shakes the excess water from his hair. After placing his tools in one of the cabinets he looks up and is startled to see her watching him.

"You scared me. I didn't see you there," he says.

"I've opened the wine."

"I see. That's good. Let me get out of these wet things and I'll join you in a glass."

"Go ahead," she quietly says.

"What?"

"I said go ahead. Take them off."

He stares at her a second, taking notice of her devilish grin. He returns her smile but says nothing. He slowly pulls down on each sleeve freeing his arms before grabbing the back collar and pulling the top over his head. He tosses it in the corner with the cap as he quickly passes his hand through his hair in an attempt to brush it from his face. He stops and looks at her for a moment, knowing that she is admiring his chiseled chest.

She remains on the lower step. "Continue," she says as she nonchalantly takes a sip of wine.

His heart quickens and his body reacts in anticipation of what is coming. He grabs the legs of the wetsuit at the thigh and pushes down the pants. They slide easily pass his narrow hips exposing his small skin tight swimsuit. He kicks them toward the corner and again stops and watches her stare.

"Oh, my goodness! I had no idea. What have I gotten myself into?" she grins and asks as she sees that the skimpy swimsuit is not having much luck covering his manhood.

He laughs and slowly begins to remove it.

She quickly raises her hand in a 'stop' signal and says, "No! Slow down. Not so fast!"

He audibly heaves a sigh as he halts the further loosening of the draw string. Between heavy breaths, he manages to say, "I'm dying here, Maggie! I need you. It's my turn. Step down into the cabin. I'm coming in!"

"That's right. That's the idea."

"He grins and softly says, "Funny. Sit on the edge of the bed and lie back."

He continues to stand tall as she slowly sits down as ordered. However, before laying back, she grabs the drawstring and slowly slides the suit down his muscular thighs. He lowers it completely and kicks it to a corner. "That's better. Now what do you want me to do?" she asks.

As he climbs in the berth beside her, he says, barely above a whisper, "Honey, I just want you to lie back and relax. Scoot as far back as you can. I'll do the rest."

Kneeling next to her reclined body he begins to unzip her flannel sweatshirt. He slowly lowers the zipper exposing her frilly bra. He smiles at the lace trim as he continues to the end. He folds back each side of the sweatshirt and admires her trim abdomen and her petite navel. He kisses it ever so slightly. She sighs.

"I'll roll over on my side and you can pull the sweatshirt off," she says.

Without a word he does as she suggested which allows him to reach behind her back and unhook the bra clasp. He gently pushes her back down.

In silence he lifts her bra over her raised arms and frees her bountiful and firm breast.

She says, "Oh, Rick. Please hurry, I don't know if I can go much longer. I have to have you."

"I bet you can." After a brief moment he bends forward and kisses her lips and then each breast. He reaches for her glass of wine and hands it to her. She props herself up on one elbow and takes a quick sip after which she offers it to him. Before setting it down, he takes a swallow. Without a word he gently pushes her back. He feels her flat stomach rise and fall rapidly as he places his hands over her navel. He moves to between her feet and reaches for her waistband. She brings her knees up and arches her back allowing him to slowly remove the loose fitting sweatpants. He does so meticulously. She arches her back again and lowers her panties to her thighs. He removes them completely then pauses as he admires her beauty.

"Oh my God!" she says.

+ + + +

They lie breathless until she says, "That was incredible."

"You are incredible," he replies.

CHAPTER NINETEEN

Six Weeks Before The Incident
Friday, February 8, 2013 at 6:00 PM

Maggie drives along in a near trance thinking of Rick. She can't get him out of her mind. She smiles to herself as she recalls the fantastic love making on the boat last weekend but frowns knowing what she has to do now. She realizes it's necessary but she still feels guilty. She dreads what she'll need to say and how she'll need to act. She can't shake the feeling that she is going to betray him even though she realizes this will lead to her ultimately being with her true love for a life time.

"This was a great idea. What made you think of it?" Justin asks, shocking her out of her dream state.

Shaking out the cobwebs and regaining her bearings, she says, "Well, lately you and I haven't been able to be alone much. Abby always seems to be the center of attention."

"You goddamn right about that!" he interrupts emphatically.

"I've wanted to do something like this for quite a while. When I discovered that one of our new neighbors has a teenage girl who baby sits, I asked her if she would be interested in sitting for Abby over night. She checked with her mother and she said sure but she would rather they stay at their house. I said fantastic. So here we are!"

"Well thank you, My Sweet! A night alone with you in a condo on the beach in Gulf Shores! I can't wait to get there. But, why Gulf Shores? We live in Pensacola Beach now," he asks.

"I just wanted to return to our old stomping grounds. We haven't been back since we moved a couple of months ago. We know the good restaurants and entertainment places around there. And we don't have to go to some kid friendly joint," she explains.

"Without that brat we could do this more often," he mutters under his breath.

"What was that? I couldn't hear what you said," she asks as she continues driving.

"Oh, nothing, just mumbling," he answers in a clear voice.

She lied; she could hear what he said. She heard it clearly and without a doubt. She couldn't believe her ears. She smiles to herself while thinking . . . that this is going to be easier than she expected.

Riding the elevator up to their floor, Maggie says, "The first one naked and under the sheets wins the prize!"

Justin turns with an astonished look and stutters, "Wa, wat, what's the prize?"

"The winner gets to screw the loser."

"My kind of game," he laughs.

+ + + +

Returning to the condo after a dinner of raw oysters on the half shell followed by dancing and one too many boilermakers, Justin says, as he falls across the bed, "Wow! What a night!"

"Yeah, it was fun. You were fun," she says as she slides open the balcony's heavy, hurricane proof doors.

"Why don't you come out here and listen to the waves breaking; it's incredible!"

As he approaches, she hears him pop open another can of beer. While rearranges a couple of damp plastic lounge chairs she asks, "Did you bring me one?"

"No. There's more in the ice chest. Go get your ass one," he says with a rather sharp tone that she didn't expect.

She bites her lip, fighting to keep from responding while thinking . . . this guy keeps reinforcing why he has to get out of my life. It's getting easier and easier to follow through with my plan.

"Turn off all the lights and come out here. There's a lounge chair. Come sit next to me," she says with as pleasant a tone as she could muster.

"Dang, it's dark out here! Can't see my goddamn hand in front of my goddamn face," he says.

"I had fun tonight Justin. I had forgotten how much fun you can be. We never seem to have enough time alone. . . . Give me your hand," she says.

"What?"

"Your hand; give it to me."

"What? Why?" he asks again as she takes his hand and places it between her legs. He reacts with a shudder as he discovers that she has removed her clothing from the waist down. He doesn't make a sound or move a muscle until he softly says, "Maggie, do you know how much I love you? I know I haven't told you that very much but I do truly love your ass."

"I know that, Justin."

"I truly truly love you," he repeats. "I can't believe that I am so lucky to have a woman like you. It just makes me all excited inside to know that I will always have you; that you will always be with me right up until the day I die; that you will always be mine."

"I know."

"Do you really? Do you really know that, Maggie? Sometimes I get the feeling that you're not so sure. I will do anything to prove it; to prove my love for you. Just say the word. Just ask me; you'll see," he pleads.

"I feel the same way Justin; just you and me."

"Do you? I often get the impression that you just tolerate me."

"Let's go get in the bed and I'll see how long you can tolerate me. Then, if you have anything left, you can show me exactly how you feel."

Maggie is thankful that it is so dark. She wouldn't want Justin to see the look of disgust on her face.

CHAPTER TWENTY

Six Weeks Before The Incident
Saturday, February 8, 2013 at 10:00 AM

"Wow, Maggie, My Sweet. You've never woke me up like that before. What's gotten into you?"

"You did!" she answers with a false laugh, then continues, "I don't really know. I guess being alone with you makes me feel free. I feel that I can do anything. I saw you lying there and I wanted to make love. I wanted it right then. I'm, that is, we're free to do what we want when we want, so I did," she answers.

"I feel the same," he says with a broad grin.

"I don't even think of Abby when we're alone. . . . Justin, you've got my head spinning. I just feel like jumping up and down naked in the middle of the bed just because I can. I feel like I can make as much noise as I want while making love to you just because I can. I, we, can't do that with Abby around."

She sees his body language and knows he is picking up on her message. She turns around so as not to face him because she wants to take a chance and ask him the ultimate question. "Justin, isn't there anything we could do that would assure that it would be just the two of us?"

He doesn't answer and she can't see his reaction.

CHAPTER TWENTY-ONE

Six Weeks Before The Incident
Saturday, February 8, 2013 at 1:00 PM

"Justin, you've been so quiet these last couple of hours; why? Is something wrong?"

"Nothing's wrong," he answers.

"Now that we've checked out, let's go walk on the pier before heading home; you know, like we use to do. We can watch the fishermen. It will make the day longer. I really don't want it to end," she suggests.

"That's fine."

+ + + +

"These parents letting their little kids sit up on that top rail and dangle their feet over scares the hell out of me. Even though they are standing behind the kid, just a slight slip and they hit the water twenty-some feet below," Maggie points out.

Justin doesn't comment at first but after staring at this one particular little girl, he says, "There is something I can do."

"What?"

"You asked if there is some way we could be alone. There is! There can be an accident! Here on this goddamn pier; Abby can meet with an accident. She can slip off the rail!" he excitedly says.

Maggie, knowing that for show she must protest vigorously, shouts, "Are you crazy? What the hell are you talking about?"

"Look Baby! Look at that little girl. That could be Abby. I could bring her here. Look around; no one's paying any attention to that girl sitting up there. She could slip back and no one would even know except the guy with her, and that would be me."

"You must have lost your mind!"

"No, look! Look at how easy it would be."

"Oh, Justin. That's a horrible thought," she says in a more normal voice.

"But our asses would be alone to do everything we've talked about this weekend."

"I realize that and it would be wonderful. . . . But poor Abby," she says as she lowers her head as if she's ashamed to even be considering such a thing.

"Think of us, My Sweet. Think of us now and in the goddamn future. Just us two doing what we want with nothing or anybody holding us back. Just think about it," he pleads.

"Oh, Justin, I don't know."

"Just think about it. Will you promise me that you will consider it?" he says as he grabs her shoulders and looks into her eyes. "I love you, Maggie. I'll do anything."

After a long silence she says, "Okay. I'll consider it. I will," she says while thinking with a hidden internal smile . . . step number one of my plan has been a complete success.

CHAPTER TWENTY-TWO

Three Weeks Before The Incident
Friday, March 1, 2013 at 3:00 PM

"Hello, my Miss Maggie. I missed seeing you here in the library this week. Where have you been hiding? Did I scare you off after our little episode on the boat?" he asks with a grin as he restlessly stands at her table. She hasn't detected this sort of edginess in him before.

"Scare me? No you didn't scare me. You did everything else to me, but scare me was not one of them," she laughs. Then she continues, "I've been busy with Abby and with these damn midterms. I had a load of papers to turn in."

"Yeah, same here. There's been a problem with Abby?" he asks. Again she sees that he is a little jittery.

"No, not directly with Abby; more with the guy I live with, Justin. But I don't want to talk about it."

"Well good, because there's something I want to talk about," he says after clearing his throat.

"Oh, yeah! What?" Is that why you're so fidgety?" she asks with an adoring smile brought on by his boyish actions.

A full thirty seconds passes before Maggie breaks the silence, "Rick, are you okay? What is it?"

"Until I met you I have never been able to put three very important words together."

"What are you talking about?" she asks with a grin.

"I and love and you are the three words. . . . I love you!" he blurts out loudly and without caring who else hears. "I love you; I love you! I . . . love . . . you! I don't know if I said it enough the other day on the boat, or if I even said it at all. I love you!"

"Rick," she whispers with a wide smile as she tugs on his sleeve. "Sit down."

"It doesn't matter who hears me. I . . . love . . . you!" he continues saying as he slowly does take a seat. "I haven't slept, I haven't eaten, I don't believe I even breathe like I use to; I find myself gasping for air. Then this horrible thought enters by messed-up brain; a thought that you might not feel the same way as I do. Then I get nauseous."

Placing her hand on his she says, "Relax my sweet, adorable, gorgeous man-child. There is no need for antacids. I love you too. On the boat you said 'I love you, Maggie' and I said 'I love you, Richard.' I didn't say it as a result of the heat of the moment. I loved you the minute you asked me if you could sit at my table. You told me when we were making love and I told you. We were pretty busy at the time so I guess you didn't remember."

"Oh, my! Oh, my! This is fantastic. I love you and you love me! This is fantastic!" he repeats.

She laughs as she leans over and kisses his temple. She sees how happy he is; how proud he is. They sit in silence and just stare at each other. At this moment no one else exists in the world.

Maggie begins gathering her books and papers. Standing to leave she says," Rick, My Love, I have to get home. When can I see you again? There're lots of things I want to say to you and something special I want to ask you."

"Yeah; me too. What about tomorrow morning. My boss wants me to go run the boat; to make sure everything is in tip-top shape. Would you mind meeting me there again?" he asks with a devilish grin.

She laughs out loud, kisses him on the cheek, and says, "I'll see you at eleven. Get ready!"

CHAPTER TWENTY-THREE

Three Weeks Before The Incident
Saturday, March 2, 2013 at 4:00 PM

Lying back breathless Maggie says, "My God, Rick! Where did you ever learn to make love like that? My toes are still curled while my insides feel totally at ease."

"I read a lot," he laughs. "My toes are fanned out like a peacock's tail and my outsides are still at attention."

Giggling, they embrace and roll over again.

+ + + +

"I can see that you surely do enjoy this boat? You just love being out on the water don't you, Rick?"

"You've got that right, My Lovely. Up until the time I met you, my favorite thing about her was everything about her. I love driving her. I love working on her motors. I love washing her down after an offshore trip. I love cleaning her bottom," he pauses and snickers. "But, since I met you, I love her sleeping berth the most," he laughs.

"The boat is female?"

"You bet she is! I make love to her every time I'm aboard. I've told you before; my goal in life is to own a boat like this and a dive shop. If I ever reach those goals, I'll be a proud and happy man. The only thing that would add to that would be you. I do so love you, Maggie."

"Rick, I'll be there if you want me."

"Why in the world wouldn't I want you?" he asks.

"Because I'm going to ask you to do something that will sound strange," she says. "From your view point, it's going to come right out of the blue. You're going to think that I've lost my ever-loving mind. There's a chance that you won't have anything further to do with me after I ask you."

"Maggie, what the hell are you talking about? I'll do anything for you. You know that; unless you want me to murder someone. I'm going to have to draw the line there," he laughs.

Maggie doesn't laugh but looks straight into his eyes.

"Oh my God! You want me to kill somebody. Are you crazy?" he shouts.

"No! No! I don't want you to kill anybody. In fact I want you to save somebody."

"Alright, Maggie; what the hell is going on? Tell me everything," he calmly says.

+ + + +

After explaining her plan to him he says, "It'll never work. And where did you get such an idiotic idea?"

"It will work and it hit me after I met you; when I learned about your swimming and diving experience and when I remembered the pier in Gulf Shores. That's when it all came together. It was reinforced when I learned of your access to the boat and to the underwater equipment," she explains.

"You want me to be at the exact spot at the exact time Justin throws your baby Abby off a pier. Then you want me to dive in and rescue her before she drowns. You are at the top of the class in love making Maggie, but I believe the rest of your brain function is way below average. Abby will drown! She will go straight to the bottom and be gone!" he yells. "Count me out!"

"She won't drown. She'll be alright," she calmly says.

"What possible reason do you have for saying that? She is barely five years old. She will die Maggie! Have you lost your mind?"

"I've been giving her diving lessons for the last six weeks or so. I found a club outside of Pensacola that teaches competitive platform diving. She loves it. She's a real dare devil. She doesn't dive but she jumps. She jumps off of the ten meter platform and swims to the side. She's fantastic. That's thirty-three feet down. Her coaches and the other kids practicing can't believe her. They marvel at her. The pier is only twenty feet above the water."

Rick looks at her in stunned disbelief and says, "You're telling me that a five year old climbs a steep ladder all the way up to a ten meter platform, jumps off that platform, goes under the water, and swims to the side of the pool?"

"That's right."

"I don't believe it. How far can she swim?" he asks.

"Believe it! She can dog paddle the length of the pool and back. The pool is twenty-five yards long. I also taught her how to do that."

"Consider me a doubting Thomas, but I'd have to see it with my own eyes," he says firmly.

"That's not a problem. I can arrange it as long as you don't let her see you."

"I'm having a hard time understanding why I'm actually having this conversation but can you please explain to me why can't she see me?"

"Because, I don't want her to recognize her rescuer. When you and I get together afterwards I don't want her confused. There will probably be several news media people wanting to interview me and her and I don't want her pointing you out."

"Unbelievable! You've really thought this out. You're serious aren't you?"

"You bet your beautiful body I am," she sternly says.

"Is that the same reason you want me to disappear; because of the media?"

"That's right. You know I want to be with you as soon as possible after the incident. I love you. If you are some sort of hero, and if the media happens to visit my house and sees you there shortly after the incident, some of them, and maybe even the police, might get suspicious. And also, I don't think that you should call me for a day or so after. Use a land line and call me at my work; don't call my cell phone," she explains.

"Suspicious of what? Suspicious of me? I just saved a little girl."

"Fraud. There's going to be very large insurance settlement because I'm going to sue the crap out of Gulf Pier that is owned and operated by the good state of Alabama."

"I thought this was about getting Justin out; not about money."

"I just think, for all our troubles, a little cash wouldn't hurt. Alabama has lots of money."

"Okay, let me see if I can summarize this mess. You get Justin to throw Abby off the pier. I jump over and save her. I disappear and my body is never found. Justin is easily arrested because he's a fool. Abby is returned to you. I return to my normal life and we, after a short time, live together happily ever after, just like in the fairy tales."

"That's it," she says.

"You get Justin out of your life, get me in your life, and put a big pile of money in your bank account," he says.

"That's right. Plus you get me, your dive shop, and that dive boat you've always wanted."

"Count me out! I don't want anything to do with it," he states as he jumps off the boat, hurries into his car, and drives away without ever looking back.

Maggie sits stunned as tears well up in her eyes.

CHAPTER TWENTY-FOUR

Two & Half Weeks Before The Incident
Wednesday, March 6, 2013 at 8:00 PM

"Justin, where is Abby?" Maggie asks as she returns from class.

"I don't know. In the back yard I think," he answers while sipping on a beer.

"In the back yard?" she yells. "It's cold outside, and it's dark. How long has she been out there?"

"Hell, I don't know. The brat wanted out so I let her out. She'll come in when she gets cold enough," he nonchalantly says.

"You son of a bitch!" Maggie shouts as she runs to the back yard. She finds Abby sitting on the lower step and asks her, "Abby baby, are you okay? Are you cold? Why didn't you come back in?"

"I tried but I couldn't reach the handle. I guess Justin didn't hear me knock so I just sat here and waited for you."

"Oh, Baby; I'm so sorry. It won't happen again." She bends down and lifts Abby into her arms. Abby squeezes her neck as she carries her back inside. Putting her down she says, "Go get into your pajamas and crawl in bed. I'll be there to tuck you in in just a minute."

She approaches Justin and says firmly but not overly loud, "Get your lazy ass up and out of my house!"

Glancing up at her, he arrogantly says, "Now, Maggie, we've been down this road already. And like before, I'm not going anywhere. Now go get me another beer!"

"Get your own beer and go, damnit!"

"I don't know what you're so upset about. Just a few days ago it was Abby who you wanted to go. Make up your damn mind. I've made up mine; I'm not leaving. Like you said, it's too cold out," he laughs.

"You bastard!"

"You seem to be forgetting how I pleasured you over and over that weekend. You liked it and you know you liked it. You chose me. Not her. Remember? Remember our plan? That plan is going to happen! Now go get me my beer and then go get your clothes off and get in bed. I'm extra horny tonight and I'm going to screw your brains out!"

"You're disgusting."

"You'll like it. You always do."

CHAPTER TWENTY-FIVE

Two Weeks Before The Incident
Friday, March 8, 2013 at 3:00 PM

"Hi, Rick; I was hoping you'd be here," Maggie says as she walks up to his table.

He stands and says, "I made a point to be. You're usually here on Fridays and I wanted to see you and to talk to you. I wanted to tell you how sorry I am for leaving you like that last weekend. I had no call to act like that; I'm sorry. Please sit down."

He pulls out a chair and motions for her sit. He returns to his in silence.

"There's no need to be. I put too much on your shoulders. I'm the one who is sorry," she says.

"Enough of that; why did you want to see me?" he asks returning to his normal upbeat manner.

"What?"

"You said that you were hoping to see me. Why? . . . What's wrong? You don't look like your usual self; you look as if you are a thousand miles away."

"I wanted to tell you that I am dropping out of school," she says while fighting back tears.

"Why? What happened?"

"Justin pulled another one of his episodes. I have to pick Abby up after her school. I can't trust him to do it and take care of her until I get home," she explains wiping her eyes.

"That bastard!" he says.

"Yeah, it's pretty bad," she continues.

"Did you tell him to leave?"

Looking at him directly she says sternly, "Rick, I've told him hundreds of time to get the hell out! He won't go! That's why I came up with that absurd plan. The only other thing I can do, besides sneaking out and relocating to another town, is knock him in the head with something the next time he forces himself on me. If I do that, I'll be the one going to jail and my little Abby will be sent to God only knows where."

"He's raping you?" he shouts as he jumps out of his chair. He paces up and down and around the table before sitting down; this time in a different chair.

"I don't know if it is technically rape. The little worm doesn't physically force me but I don't have a choice in the matter. I don't fight it," she cries.

"Oh, Maggie. My sweet sweet Maggie," he softly says as he too cries shamelessly.

Maggie wipes her eyes, stands, and says as she prepares to leave, "Well, I just wanted to let you know that I'm dropping out."

"Wait!" he says after drying his eyes with the back of his hand. . . . "When can I see Abby go off the ten meter platform?"

Maggie, taken aback, pauses and asks, "You mean you'll do it?"

"I want you to have someone push her off without her being aware. No goggles, no swimsuit, just her everyday clothing," he says.

"Rick, does that mean you'll do it?" she repeats.

"I want to see how she reacts. Then I'll decide."

"I'll let you know the time and place. I'm shooting for tomorrow. Would that work out with you?"

"That'd be fine," he calmly says.

She excitedly kisses him and leaves with a broad smile. She's about to see part two and part three of her plan come about; preparing Abby and persuading Rick.

CHAPTER TWENTY-SIX

Two Weeks Before The Incident
Saturday, March 9, 2013 at 11:00 AM

As planned, Rick arrives at the training facility thirty minutes before Maggie and Abby are scheduled to show. He locates a set of bleachers that will give him a perfect view of the platform. He stands in the shadows of those bleachers and watches as the two of them climb the ladder up to the ten meter level; Maggie following close behind her daughter. Earlier Maggie had asked her if she would show her what it looked like from up there. Upon reaching the top he watches as Abby boldly approaches the edge, stops and signals for her mother to come look. He watches as Maggie fakes a stumble, bumps into Abby, and knocks her off the platform. He grimaces as he hears Abby's shriek and sees her out-of-control fall toward the water thirty-three feet below. He watches as she helplessly hits at an awkward angle, mainly landing on her back and side. He watches with bated breath as she disappears with a not-so-large splash under the water. Out of the corner of his eye, he sees Maggie scurrying down the ladder. Breathless for several seconds, he watches in amazement as Abby pops to the surface. He watches as she cries out for help before she steadies herself by wiping her long golden hair from her face. He's astonished as he watches her easily dog paddle to the edge.

Maggie reaches her and says, as she helps her out of the pool, "Oh, my baby; I'm so sorry. Are you okay?"

"Yes, Mommy, I'm okay," she says, even managing a slight grin.

Maggie is amazed by her brave daughter. She stands erect and faces the bleachers and signals a thumbs-up indicating Abby's fine. Rick nods then smiles to himself as he exits through a side entrance. His inner smile ceases with the realization of the reality of his task ahead.

CHAPTER TWENTY-SEVEN

Two Weeks Before The Incident
Sunday, March 10, 2013 at 2:00 PM

Maggie calls out from the kitchen as she hears a hard, repeated knock at her front door, "Who is it? I'm coming; hold your horses!"

She's startled as she opens the door and sees a large, uniformed police officer standing and gripping the left bicep of a hand cuffed Justin. She notices a stupid meek look on Justin's face as the officer says, "Sorry to bother you, Ma'am, I'm Officer Jackson. This fellow says he lives here. Is that the case?"

"Yes, yes he lives here. His name Is Justin Webb. What did he do?" she asks disgustedly.

"I'll let him tell you the details. I was going to arrest him up by the school but he begged me not to. He cried like a baby. I agreed to let him off if he could show me some proof of a stable home and that he is employed. Does he have a regular job, Ma'am?"

"Yes; as of Friday he's been working steady. I guess it's been two or three months."

"How long has he lived here with you?" the officer asks.

"It's been a long time; a very long time. We lived together in Gulf Shores before moving here a few months back," she answers staring at Justin with revulsion. Justin understands her expression and answers her look with his own that says . . . he doesn't care how she feels about him, he's here and he's not going anywhere.

"I understand, Ma'am. If you have any problems with him you be sure to call the police department."

"I will, thank you."

"Alright, Mr. Webb; you're free to go. If you cause any more trouble your next stop will be central lockup," Officer Jackson says as he unlocks the handcuffs.

"Thanks, Officer Jackson. You're a kind man. There will be no more trouble from me," Justin mockingly says as he jerks his arm from the officer's grip. He stares at Maggie with scorn as he enters the room.

+ + + +

"What now, Justin? What did you get into?" Maggie asks is a civil voice.

"Oh, these damn brats at school wouldn't let me play basketball with them. They said they had enough players. I just wanted to substitute. I was just taking a walk and I felt like it would be fun if I played a few minutes."

"Why on God's green earth would you want to play basketball with a bunch of kids?"

"Kids hell; these so-called kids were teenage bastards and half of them were a head taller than me," he tries to explain. "They wouldn't let me substitute so when their goddamn ball rolled towards me I threw it across the street. It just so happened that the damn thing kept bouncing and rolling until it ended up in the canal. They couldn't reach it so the next thing I know that stupid cop shows up."

"You can't mind your own business, can you Justin? I've told you before that you want attention. Attention that gets you into trouble. As I said then, I don't think you can help it; that you like to get caught. However, like I also said back then, I guess that's what I like about you," she says with a broad forced grin that hurts her to her soul.

"And, as I said before, bull shit!" he exclaims. Although it was quite a thrill riding in the back of that police car. That's the first time I've done that. . . . By the way, where is Abby? I haven't heard her since I've been back."

"She's next door visiting that little baby sitter."

"Really! Let's get naked. How long will she be gone?" he asks hungrily as he begins stripping down.

Maggie laughs as she too starts stripping knowing she has to play her part to the end. "She'll be gone at least an hour. Let's get to it!"

+ + + +

Lying naked and uncovered as Justin slips on his pants, Maggie says, "Wow, Justin! You were pretty good."

"Yeah, I was, wasn't I?"

Maggie continues as she places her hands behind her head, not making any effort to cover herself, "These are the good times we want. These are the good feelings we want. Making love to you is fun and it feels soooo goood! That's why I get so annoyed with you when you play around with fire."

"Fire? What the hell are you taking about now? I need a beer!" he says.

"When you constantly get in trouble," Maggie says. "When we go and do with Abby what we discussed, it is very important, extremely important, that you do not stand out. You can't take any chances just for the thrill of it. If you get caught, we will never be together. Like today; why not just enjoy your walk? No, you have to join in. Well, if you act like that on *that* day with Abby, you're going to go to jail! You can't stand out! You have to act like an average person! You must blend in! Do you understand?"

"I understand; I understand! Blend in! Damnit, how many times are you going to say it? Get up and get dressed! You look nasty lying flat on your back all open like that," he says as he walks away to get his beer.

CHAPTER TWENTY-EIGHT

Ten Days Before The Incident
Wednesday, March 13, 2013 at 11:00 AM

Meeting at their predetermined location, their table in the library, Rick says, "Well, that was quite a show your little Abby put on the other day. She's some trooper."

"You liked that? I thought you'd be impressed. I figure, since you have shown up here, that you are going to help me get rid of Justin," Maggie says with a grateful smile.

"I'm going to help you get him out of your life. I'm not going to get rid of him," he says with a serious expression.

"Of course! I'm sorry I put it that way. . . . You know that you look super handsome when you get serious; a lot sexier too."

He smiles and says, "I'm trying to be serious here, Maggie. But you're so gorgeous and I love you so much, all I want to do is lay you back across this table and make passionate love to you."

"Well, Mr. Rick, the day's young. I'm sure something can be arranged to relieve your wants a little later but right now we have to discuss the details. Have you come up with your part of the plan?" she asks.

"Of course! Now can we go? It's a little later," he says as he fakes getting out of his chair.

"I'm serious, Rick. We have to talk about this," she begs with an ever so slight grin. "I want to understand it all."

"I know, I know."

"Well! Tell me! Go ahead; what's your plan?"

"Yesterday, I made a trip to Gulf Shores and scouted out the pier as well as the surrounding area. I saw that the water is quite clear but not too clear, which is perfect for what I want to do. I estimate that I will be able to see anywhere from eight to ten feet. The fishermen I talked to said the water is about thirty feet deep at the end of the pier and that it drops off rather slowly from there. So that's good. I was worried that if it got too deep too quick, that could pose a problem."

"Why would that be a problem?" she asks.

"A few days before the happening, I am going to have to hide some equipment a good distance from the pier. With this gear I will be able to swim far enough away and be sure that I won't be spotted when I surface. I have to do this because you won't let me bask in the hero spotlight," he says teasing her.

"I told you why we must do it that way," she says. "We will be together! It's just risky to do so too soon. . . . I love you, Rick. It will only be about a month. That should be enough time."

"I know and I understand the logic. I guess I can live with that. I always wanted to be a hero though," he kids.

"Alright, Captain America, continue. Tell me about this gear and equipment."

"I'm going to wear a pair of cargo type pants with lots of pockets. All my items will fit nicely in them. I'll be carrying a hand held extra air device, a folding knife, a small mask, and special designed ear plugs. I altered the mask so that it's easier to use the air device and to clear the water from the mask, when I'm underwater."

"I see; why ear plugs?"

"They are actually a receiver. I will have planted a tracking beeper in with the equipment I mentioned earlier. This little receiver will lead me right to them saving me time, therefore saving me air. . . . I love you, Maggie."

They smile at each other as she says, "Tell me about this equipment."

"I'm going to have a wetsuit since the water temp is going to be in the mid to high fifties, which is cold. Once I get it on, which is going to be problem under water, but I've done it before, I'll strap on a rebreather."

"What the heck is a rebreather?" she asks.

"It's like the regular scuba gear but you don't have tanks. You use your own air over and over. You don't release any air bubbles. It's really neat. Then I'm going to fire up the DPD. That's as in Diver Propulsion Device. It's like a little torpedo that I'll hang on to and it will pull me far away from the area faster than I can swim. I scouted a deserted beach in a national park that's about three miles away and that's where I get out. The morning of, I'll park my car there and pretend I'm out for a jog and go to the pier. It'll be a short walk back to my car from the surf. Nobody should be around, but even if they are it's nothing out of the ordinary to see a diver on the beach."

"You are amazing!" she says. "So you are okay with all of this? If you are, can we go make love now? I'm about to explode!"

"It's not a hundred percent guarantee that my scheme will work, but for you I'll take the chance even if it's only ten percent. Don't light your fuse just yet, let me do that," he says as they each stand and begin walking.

"Where are we going? It's too far to the boat."

"I have a classmate who lets me use his apartment. It's within walking distance and he's out of town until tomorrow," he announces with glee.

"Walk hell, let's run!" she shouts.

+ + + +

Lying naked and uncovered side by side, Maggie says, "Wow Rick! How do you do that? You come up with something new every time we make love. You are truly incredible."

"It's not me, it's you my love. I just want to show you how much I love you. I want you to experience as must pleasure as possible." He grabs her hand and holds it in silence for several minutes after which he sits up, looks at her and says, "Please don't move. You look so beautiful lying back like that."

Maggie laughs to herself as she remembers Justin's reaction three days ago to a similar situation. Regrettably she rolls over and puts her feet on the floor as she says, "Oh, Baby, I'd love to stay like that all day and have you watch me but I have to get up and go get Abby from school."

"Oh, pooh; you're no fun," he teases. "When do me meet again and get this program moving? I'm going to need a few days to gather and set up everything."

"Next Monday, same table at the library, at nine-thirty. I'm aiming for the weekend after that."

"That'll work for me. Give me a kiss and I'll see you Monday," he says.

CHAPTER TWENTY-NINE

Five Days Before The Incident
Monday, March 18, 2013 at 9:30 AM

At the library, Rick says, "Maggie, there's only one thing I'm still hung up on."

"What's that?"

"If Justin doesn't get caught then this whole exercise is for nothing. I'll pop out of the water and learn that he is back living with you and Abby. You lose because he's still there and I lose because I'm not. Nothing was accomplished. How are you so sure this idiot will get caught?" he asks with serious concern.

"Because he's just that, an idiot. He loves to live on the edge; especially when there is a chance of getting police involved. It's in his little brain. He told me just the other day that he was thrilled to finally ride in the back of a police car. He got into a fight over a basketball game with some fifteen year olds. He's nuts."

"That's what you are basing this on; a basketball game?"

"He likes to stand out. He does not and will not blend in with the crowd. He goes to the store to pick up some milk and steals a jar of peanut butter by placing it under a skin tight tee shirt. It was bulging so much the clerk probably could read the label. He knew there was a chance the cops would come. He gets into a fight with a little boy's mother at the park because he pushes him aside. The cops come again. He fights with a teacher at Abby's school. Again the cops are involved. He will do something just as dumb and stupid on the pier or shortly thereafter. Trust me; he will get caught."

"Well okay. I guess you're right," Rick reluctantly says.

"I'll give you half of the insurance award if he doesn't. Heck, I'll give you seventy-five percent. You can go and buy your boat and set up your dive shop. . . . He will get caught!" she insists.

"I'm not in this for the money. I'm in this for you!" he shouts, forgetting for a moment that he's in the library filled with many people. He nervously looks around and sees that only a few appear to be interested in what was said. Looking back at Maggie he whispers, "I'm in this for you; just for you."

She places her hand on his, saying, "I know you are darling. Everything is going to work out. You'll see. . . . If not, I'll hit him in the back of the head with my brand new cast iron frying pan."

Rick looks at her and sees a wide smile. He relieved to see that she was only kidding. Then he asks, "Okay, what's next on the agenda?"

"I've been watching the weather and the weekend is shaping up to be ideal conditions. Winds should be calm after the passage of a cool front. Of course that's five days out and that could change. I'm not planning to mention it to Justin until Wednesday. The weather will tell the tale then."

"So, as of right now, the day is this coming Saturday. Is that right?" he asks.

"That's it."

"I'll go out this evening and place the equipment. If for some reason it's not this weekend I can always go and retrieve it."

"Sounds like a plan. Be careful tonight," she says as she leans back in her chair completely relaxed realizing that all the details are in place. She lowers her head slightly, inhales deeply then releases a long, audible breath as if the load on her back and shoulders has finally been removed.

Rick stands and walks around to her chair and lifts her chin. He kisses her moist lips with a long but soft loving touch. "You'll call me Wednesday whether it's a go or no go, right?" he asks still holding her chin.

Touching his hand she answers, "That's right, Honey. I'll also give you the time. I'll schedule you to be at the pier thirty minutes before Abby and Justin, just to make sure he doesn't go ahead with it without you being there. I won't let them leave the house too early. That will be more assurance against that happening."

"Well, my boss has me pretty tied up the rest of this week so I guess I won't see you for four or five weeks," he solemnly says.

Don't think of it like that. Think of us at the end of that time. It will be glorious!" she shouts throwing her arms into the air and not caring who is listening or watching. "Glorious!"

Rick laughs, gives her a quick but loving kiss, turns and walks away.

He never looks back. She sees him wipe his eyes.

CHAPTER THIRTY

Three Days Before The Incident
Wednesday, March 20, 2013 at 6:00 PM

After checking the local weather forecast on the computer, Maggie calls from the kitchen, "Justin, will you come here a second?"

"What for? I'm watching the end of 'Strange People.' It's a new reality show. For kicks these weirdoes are going around their neighborhood carrying a ladder and climbing up on their neighbor's roofs and stomping around until the people come out. They film the reaction of the home owners. It's hilarious. I think the weirdoes get the crap beat out of them at the end of the show. I want to see that," he shouts.

"I have something I want to tell you."

Aggravated he says, "Alright, alright, I'm coming. What is it? Hurry, I want to watch it."

"I want you to take Abby on the outing to the pier this weekend, Saturday," she states.

He stares at her for a few seconds before asking, "Are you sure?"

"Yes. It takes about an hour to drive so if you leave here by nine-thirty that will give you a lot of time to get there. You should be able to get back by mid afternoon. I'll be here waiting for you," she says with her practiced grin.

"I'll leave at nine," he excitedly says.

"That's fine. I can probably get Abby ready by then; breakfast and all. I won't be able to do it any sooner," she calmly says even though her insides are nothing but a jumble of nerves.

"Be ready Saturday afternoon when I walk in the door. We are going to do some serious damn celebrating. As a matter of fact, I think you ought to be naked. Yeah, you should be stark naked the first time I see you; right when I walk in. And, you should wear your high heels. Naked women look awesome in high heels. You could even be carrying a beer for me. Wow, that's going to be fantastic! I'm getting aroused just thinking about it. Let's screw now! A pre-celebration." Remembering his show, he slaps his forehead and runs to the TV, shouting, "Oh, crap! I missed the end. I wanted to see the asshole get beat up. Damnit!"

"It'll be rerun. I'm sure you'll catch it then," Maggie sarcastically yells. Thinking and smiling to herself . . . I'm sure they will run it many times in the recreational room of the state pen.

CHAPTER THIRTY-ONE

Morning of The Incident
Saturday, March 23, 2013 at 9:00 AM

Aware that heavy clothing will weight her down, Maggie picks out a light summer outfit for Abby. It is one of her daughter's favorites and she eagerly helps her mother with the buttons. She looks up and sees Maggie wipe a tear. "What's the matter, Mommy? Are you crying?"

"No, baby, I'm just getting a cold. That's why I'm not going with you and Justin today. I'll see you this afternoon," she whispers.

Justin shouts, "What's going on in there? We have to get on the road."

Maggie gives her a big hug and kisses her cheeks before calling out, "She's ready, Justin." Abby stands and returns the hugs.

After walking around a few minutes, Justin lifts Abby and sits her on the worn wooden rail with her back to the Gulf. She squirms a little to get comfortable, smiles, and looks around and down at the water as he lightly holds her tiny hands. He brushes her golden hair aside and tenderly kisses her on the forehead. She smiles again because he's never done that before. He holds the kiss as he releases her hands and nudges her just enough for her to lose her balance. She falls back, without making a sound, flailing her arms as she franticly tries to grab his hands or the railing. He glances down for only a second but long enough to see the panic on her face as she enters the water, landing on her back. The surface of the water divides with a small splash as she passes through, seals quickly over her as she submerges, and then she's gone.

With a completely unconcerned expression, keeping in mind that he must blend in, Justin begins slowly walking away. He hears a woman's scream and sees a shape run past him and dive over the rail. Unnerved, he runs.

+ + + +

Rick paces slowly around the perimeter of the octagonal end of the pier. Still carrying the hoop net, he occasionally glances at a fisherman but he never fully takes his eyes off of Justin and Abby. He notices that Justin never lets go of her hand, not even when she bends down to touch a dead king mackerel's eye. He's thinking . . . this guy is a real sleaze. What in the world did Maggie ever see in this puny, greasy, pot-head looking misfit? I ought to throw him over on my way to get Abby. That will save everybody a lot of time and expense and it definitely would make me feel better.

"Oh crap; it looks like it's show time," he mutters. . . . "Damnit, it didn't take him long; she's over. God help her!"

Rick runs pass Justin to the spot where she went over, tosses the hoop net down on the deck so that it will easily be seen by any rescuer, and sheds all clothing except his equipment laden pants. He sees Abby resurface and immediately struggle to keep her head above water. He thinks . . . she sure is a tough little gal. As planned, he vaults over the rail a good distance from her in order to be sure his splash and wave won't complicate her efforts.

Surfacing, he shakes his head, whipping his hair to remove the water from it and his eyes. He locates her only a couple of yards away and after three quick freestyle strokes he reaches her just as it appears she is losing her battle. The net splashes down at the same instant. Holding her by the arm he steadies the net with the other hand and pulls her onto it as his powerful kicks keep him up. He smiles to himself after chancing a glance up to see that Abby has made it. He's pleased and takes several slow freestyle strokes designed to let him catch his breath. He's thinking . . . I would really like to look up. I'm sure the people are watching me; watching a hero. I bet they are waving and shouting. Oh, well; Maggie's right. That would be risky. Now; back to business.

Rick takes in three gulps of precious air and dives. He knows the water is about thirty feet deep and wants to be near the bottom as he searches for his stash of life saving equipment. After about thirty to forty-five seconds of swimming, he slows and hovers a second as he pulls his mask out of one of the pockets. He slips it over his head and as soon as he clears the water he sees the grey outline of a shark in the distance. It appears to be circling, checking him out. He reaches for and pulls his knife out while thinking . . . okay big fellow. I know that I'm in your domain but I'm not ready to be a meal just yet. You just stay out there a little longer and let me suck on this air bottle a second and then, if you like, we can do battle. You seem to be zeroing in on my feet, huh? Is it all that movement catching your eye, mister shark? You see this knife? It's as sharp as any razor ever made and ten times as strong. What are you going to do? I've read that I'm supposed to punch you in the nose but I'm not so sure about that. You're one of those mean old bull sharks, aren't you? I can tell by how fat you appear to be, but I know you're only muscle and bone controlled by a peanut brain. I think it's going to take more than a poke in the nose to deter you. Isn't that right? I don't have an unlimited supply of air and I can't surface. It wouldn't do me any good anyway, because you'll attack down here or up there. Isn't that right, mister shark? So, let's get it on, or not. But, one way are the other, you aggravating hungry beast, it's going to be finished; it will be me or it will be you that swims on.

Rick turns on his back and exaggerates his kicking. The shark turns to 'take the bait' and attacks. He stops kicking and quickly pulls in his legs. This apparently confuses the hungry shark. It slows and glides up and over Rick, giving him the opportunity he was hoping for. The knife easily pierces the relatively soft underbelly, about two feet behind its mouth. Rick is able to hold on to the knife handle as the seven inch blade slices down toward its tail as it frenetically attempts to free itself from this dagger in its gut. It finally manages to escape and swims crazily out of Rick's sight, trailing a massive amount of blood.

Thinking . . . okay, it's time to get back to the task at hand. This cold is beginning to get to me. Rick folds and put the life saving knife away, draws a couple more breaths from the bottle, and inserts the ear plugs.

Immediately he hears the pinging of his sending unit. Within five minutes he's able to locate his gear. He struggles but finally manages to climb into the wetsuit. He immediately feels the remaining heat from his body begin to warm the water between the suit and his skin. He slips into the straps of the rebreather and for the first time in awhile draws in and fills his lungs with sweet tasting air. He collects all the various items and stuffs them in his handy mesh swim bag. He looks around the sea floor to see if he's left anything that might later turn out to be a clue that he was there. Satisfied, he checks the coordinates on his watch and sets the destination. He flips the switch on the DPD to the 'on' position and points it in the direction that's indicated on the watch. He grabs the handles and squeezes the throttle. Within forty-five minutes he's on the beach. He looks up at the sky, pumps his fist in celebration, and shouts, "I did it! Maggie, I did it!"

PART THREE

After The Incident

CHAPTER THIRTY-TWO

Afternoon of The Incident
Saturday, March 23, 2013 at 5:00 PM

Maggie nervously paces the floor and has been for hours. She thought she would have heard something by now. There hasn't been anything on the news; no phone calls; nothing. She sits on the edge of the couch but only briefly. She walks to the kitchen and opens the refrigerator looking for something although she doesn't know what. She sits at the kitchen table and takes a sip of cold coffee. She slams the cup down with disgust seconds before jumping to her feet as a result of hearing a forceful knock on the door. She runs across the room and flings it open with such force that is slams against the wall. She sees Abby and cries out, "Oh, baby! Where have y'all been? I was so worried!"

"Ms. James, are you Ms. Margaret James?" asks one of three female police officers standing with Abby. "I think we have something for you," she says with a smile as Abby runs into her mother's arms.

"Yes, of course! I've been worried sick. They should have been back hours ago. I didn't hear a thing. No phone call, nothing. I was so worried. I should have gone with them. Where's Justin? Please come in," she rambles.

"I'm sorry to inform you but there's been an incident."

"What? What kind of incident?" Maggie asks as she pulls Abby closer to her.

"No one has been injured. Abby has been checked over by the emergency room doctors and she is perfect; as you can see."

"What? Oh my God!" she shrieks as she checks Abby's arms and legs for any injuries.

"I think you'll find that Abby is okay," Ms. James.

Maggie notices one of the officers place a hand over her ear, apparently listening intensely to her ear piece. This officer then says, "Ms. James, a Mr. Justin Webb has just now been arrested, out in the front of your house. He is currently being transported to headquarters and will be charged with the attempted murder of your beautiful little girl."

"Oh, my; Justin? Justin did this?"

Abby looks up at her and nods her head 'yes.'

"Her hair; did it get wet or something?" she asks while running her fingers through the unkempt curls. "Where are her clothes; her favorite little outfit? Why is she dressed differently?"

"It's because she got wet, Ms. James. But perhaps Abby would like to go to her room while I tell you about it."

Maggie, in agreement, asks, "Baby, would you like to go play in your room while I finish talking to these nice people?"

Abby sprints away after Maggie puts her down.

"This information can be quite upsetting. Perhaps you take a seat."

"Sure; of course. My God! What the hell happened?" Maggie asks with a deeply concerned tone.

"There's no easy way to say this but Mr. Webb allegedly threw Abby off the pier. If it wasn't for a hero who happened to be there, she would have drowned."

At hearing the word 'hero' Maggie's insides leap with joy as she holds her hand over her mouth in mock shock. She sees Rick in her mind's eye swimming underwater to the location of the equipment. She sees him holding onto that mini torpedo as it pulls him miles from the pier. She sees him make his way through the surf and place the equipment in the trunk of his car. She sees him right now, in his apartment in Navarre, sipping on a tall glass of red wine counting down the hours to when he can call her. After a second she says, "Threw her off the pier? Are you sure? Maybe it was an accident."

"No Ma'am. We have an eye witness," one of the other officers adds.

"What about the hero? When can I get to meet him?" Maggie asks with a slight grin that's meant to signal how happy she is that someone helped Abby.

"The news about him is also quite distressing, Ms. James. It seems that he drowned, or worse. . . . His body has not been recovered."

Maggie says nothing as the phrase 'or worse' shocks her. Her heart begins to race as she realizes that she has to be smart with her next comments and her outward reactions. "Drowned? Oh, the poor man. That's horrible."

"Yes Ma'am, it is."

"Do you know his identity?" she asks. "Maybe I could thank his family." It feels as if her heart is going to tear from her chest until she gets to ask the next question.

"No Ma'am, no papers at all. He removed his jacket and shirt but not his pants before diving in. We presume his wallet was in those."

Maggie takes a deep breath and her fists unconsciously tighten, as she says, "You said, 'or worse.' What could be worse than drowning?"

"It seems the witnesses on the pier deck saw a couple of sharks; two rather large bull sharks."

"Sharks? Oh, no!"

"Yes Ma'am. There is even a report that one was following the man as he swam to the shore. Right before attacking, the swimmer dove deep in an apparent attempt to elude the shark, or sharks."

Maggie jumps to her feet. "Oh, my dear God! . . . My God!" Using all the control she can muster, she slowly sits back down and asks, in a barely audible voice," There's no sign of him?"

"Nothing Ma'am. The witnesses said there was a lot of blood after he dove under but it quickly dissipated."

Maggie stares straight ahead at nothing; remaining seated, she mutters, "Thank you officers. Thanks for bringing Abby home. I think that I would like to be alone with her now. Would you mind letting yourselves out? I need to hug my baby. I really need my baby."

CHAPTER THIRTY-THREE

Two Days After The Incident
Monday, March 25, 2013 at 9:05 AM

"I'm sorry Sir; Maggie is not going to be in today. She just called. Can someone else help you?"

"Not in? Are you sure? But we had an appointment. She's never failed to meet me. She's the only one who can cut my hair correctly."

"Like I said, I'm sorry. She called and said that she wasn't feeling well. Perhaps you could try one of our other stylists?"

"No; that's okay," A confused Rick says as he hangs up the phone. Without hesitation, traceable or not, he digs his cell phone out of his jacket and calls.

+ + + +

The vibration of the buzzing phone is nearly dampened completely by the heavy bed covers. Maggie, aroused but only to a semi-awake state, rolls over and throws her arm over her still sleeping Abby. The buzzing stops and she begins returning to a sound sleep as Abby suddenly sits up and says, "Mommy, I'm hungry. You forgot to give me my bedtime snack last night."

"Oh, okay baby. Just give me a few minutes. I can't seem to open my eyes. There's a banana and a sugar donut on the counter. You can reach them. Let me stay in bed a little longer then I'll fix you some breakfast," Maggie says, pulling the blanket over her head.

"I don't want a banana," she cries. . . . "I'm thirsty too, Mommy. I can't pour the milk; it's too heavy. . . . Mommy, are you going to stay in bed again? I thought I heard a phone. I heard a buzz, or something," she says.

"What? When; when did you hear a buzz?" Maggie asks as she rolls over to face Abby.

"I don't know. When you were sleeping; it kind-of tickled my feet."

Maggie quickly sits up and starts searching under the covers for her phone. Finding it, she struggles to turn on the screen but once she does, her heart leaps as she sees a recent missed call and recognizes Rick's number. She hesitates before redialing as the thought crosses her mind . . . what am I going to do, how am I going to react if someone other than Rick answers? She taps the number. After three excruciating rings Rick answers and says, "Hi Baby! Sorry I'm using my cell but I just had to hear your voice. How come you're not at work?"

Maggie immediately breaks down and begins sobbing. She's unable to speak. Rick says, "Maggie, what's the matter? What happened? Are you alright? Is it Abby? . . . Maggie, talk to me!"

After several seconds, which felt like minutes to Rick, she manages to say, between gradually diminishing sobs, "I'm fine, Abby's fine, everybody is fine, even you." Her audible weeping begins anew as Rick says, "Maggie, you're at home, right? Stay there. I can be there in forty-five minutes!" he exclaims.

"No! No you can't do that. We all are okay here. It was you who I was worrying about," she says having regained her composure except for an occasional sniffle. "We have to stick to our plan."

"The plan be damned! I'm coming!" he calls out again.

"It was you. You are what I was so upset about. I thought that you were dead."

"Dead? Good heavens; why would you ever think that? . . . Oh, my!"

"These police officers told me when they brought Abby home. They said there were sharks. The people saw blood; lots of blood," she explains trying to control her emotions.

"Oh, Maggie, I'm so sorry. I put you thought hell. You must have been devastated when you heard that," he softly says. "I'm so, so sorry."

"Are you okay? Did you get bitten?" she asks.

"I'm fine, my little Maggie. I don't have a scratch on me."

"What about the blood? I don't understand," she asks.

"As I was diving down and swimming toward the gear I saw, out of the corner of my eye, this big fish. I guess it was following me and I got ready just in case it attacked. When it did I stabbed it pretty good. It was all over in a second. Then I got the hell out of Dodge. That's all there was to it. I didn't see a second one. If there was, it and all of its buddies had a feast."

Rick hates not to be completely truthful with Maggie, but it wouldn't serve any purpose to give her the actual details. In fact, it may very well harm her psyche. Those particulars are something he will never forget; she doesn't need to know them, at least not now.

"Rick, I was so scared. I just knew I had lost you," she says as she again begins to cry.

"Don't cry, Baby. I'm okay; Abby's okay; and you will be okay soon."

"I know. Now that I know you're alright, I'll be fine. I don't want you to worry about me; okay?"

"I will worry about you right up to the minute I see you next month," he says. "I love you, my sweet Maggie. . . . Oh, what about Justin?"

"I love you, my Richard Rubio, and that ass is in jail. I hope I never see him, or hear from him again."

"Sounds like we did it," he says.

"I love you, Rick."

CHAPTER THIRTY-FOUR

Two Weeks After The Incident
Friday, April 5, 2013 at 7:30 PM

Steven Acer takes two steps at a time as he decides to forgo the elevator and use the alternate stairway up to the third floor. He's feeling great and excited to see Julie tonight. He hasn't really been able to spend any time with her outside of their normal workday contacts. He frequently consults with her on individual cases but it's been two weeks since that incident on the pier and they haven't been able to really have a date since then. That is until tonight. He raps his standard knock on her door and playfully follows it up with another. He continues until Julie quickly pulls it open and says, without that smile that he was expecting, "Not so loud. I have a splitting headache. Why were you banging on my door anyway? I was coming as fast as I could," she scolds.

"I'm sorry, Baby. I was just having a little fun. I'm excited to see you. It's been two weeks since we've been able to be together," he answers keeping up his smile. "Are you ready? I'm all set to boogie tonight!"

"I don't feel up to it, Steven; with this headache and all," she says.

"Oh, heck. I'm sorry to hear that. But that's okay; we can party right here. I can sit on the couch and you can rest your head on my lap. I'll massage your temples and we can watch one of those silly romance movies you like so much," he suggest with his ever present grin.

"Steven, you're so sweet but I don't think so. I would rather be alone tonight. I'm just down in the dumps," she explains.

"Really? What's the matter? Is it something you can tell me? Maybe I can help," he asks.

"No, not any one thing. I'm just tired. I imagine it's because all I see every day is death or dying. I don't think I've been the same ever since that pier thing."

"Oh, that. You should put that out of your head. The baby is fine and with her mother. The jerk is in prison and will be for a long time. The poor soul is lost but we can't do anything about that. Can we?" he asks.

"I know all that Steven. I still think about it constantly though. . . . Have you done any follow up; any additional investigation?"

"Follow up? No, there's nothing to investigate," he says confused at the question.

"It just seems weird that a guy all of a sudden tries to kill a baby; especially one he's lived with for quite a while. I don't know; it just seems strange. I for one can't get my mind around it."

"The guy said he did it because her mother wanted him and not her. He's a fool; a moron. Now, if you let me take you to bed I bet I could make you forget about everything, including that incident."

"I know you could. Believe me, I've thought about doing just that. But it wouldn't be fair to you," she says.

"Don't worry about me. I'll be fine," he laughs.

"Maybe tomorrow night. Would that be okay with you? I'm sure I'll feel up to it by then," she says.

"Okay. I can take a hint. You know of course that my body is not use to being rejected," he says. "Give me a kiss. On second thought give me two kisses. I didn't get one when I came in."

She finally smiles as she kisses him quickly and softly on each cheek. He steps back and says, "Wow. That was something. I'm not really sure what, but it was something," he says with a puzzled expression.

She opens the door and stands to the side as he leaves.

+ + + +

Julie calls the next day and leaves a message on his cell. "Steven, I'm going to pass on our date tonight. Sorry Honey, just not in the mood. Call me."

He doesn't return the call until the middle of the week.

CHAPTER THIRTY-FIVE

Four Weeks After The Incident
Saturday, April 20, 2013 at 3:00 PM

"Okay Steven, what is this master plan that you have come up with to pull me out of my doldrums?" Julie asks as he holds the car door open for her.

Bowing at the waist, he says, "Please enter my chariot, My Queen, and you'll begin to marvel at the wondrous workings of your prince as he saves you from the burning castle tower. I am, as any prince worth his salt would do, going to attack the problem head on; a frontal attack that will destroy the villains once and for all."

"What the heck does that mean?" she asks with a broad smile.

"I see that My Queen has taken it upon herself to find merriment in the forthcoming venture. That is a good omen."

"If that means what I think it means, then yes, I think you're silly and that is amusing to me," she answers maintaining the smile.

"That royal grin is proof beyond any doubt that my grand plan is beginning to work."

Julie laughs out   loud but abruptly stops as she sees Steven turn off the highway and into the pier's parking area. She doesn't comment but only lowers her head.

Steven notices her reaction but continues, "And now, to deliver the final death blow to the evil demon, the good and beautiful queen and the handsome and mighty prince shall together walk, hand in hand, along the perilous path that will lead to her liberation."

"Steven, I can't."

Exiting the car he grabs and turns her to face him, saying, "Yes you can. It's just a dumb inanimate pier made of wood and concrete, but it's full of life. It's full of people laughing and having fun. But not everybody is like that; some people do dumb and terrible things. Those people, for whatever reason, destroy. It's my job and your job to pick up the pieces of those things these idiots break."

"I don't know; I don't know if I can."

"As he offers his hand, he says with a smile that he hopes will be contagious, "It was a onetime thing and there was nothing you or I could have done to prevent it. Come on, you'll see. Let's go join the fun people."

They stop at the refreshment window and Steven orders two soft pretzels and a diet drink, thinking . . . this might keep her hands busy and maybe relax her a bit. They begin their stroll. Julie says hardly a word as they occasionally halt and watch a fisherman bait his hook and cast out. After a few more steps they join in some excitement. A young boy has apparently hooked a sizable speckled trout and he's in the process of reeling it up to the pier deck. As he swings it over the guardrail, the frantic fish manages to throw the hook and it falls to the deck. The proud boy gives a high five to an apparent sibling then proceeds to pick up the gasping trout and throw it in the ice chest. Steven sees that Julie allows herself a slight grin as they slowly continue to the end of the pier.

Julie hesitates as they reach the octagon shaped end. She knows that this is the area from which little Abby was dropped. Steven continues on to the outer-most guard rail. Stopping short of it, he stands erect as he takes deep breaths while staring out and marveling at the beauty of the horizon of the cloudless sky as it meets the distant Gulf of Mexico. He's brought out of his semi-trance by a woman's voice calling, "Detective; Detective!"

He turns and recognizes the lady but can't remember from where are when. She says as she approaches, "Hi, Detective, remember me? Sue Peters. . . Sunshine."

"Oh, yeah; hello Miss Peters. Yes, I do now. You were one of the witnesses. I remember you. It's nice to see you again. What are you doing here now? I don't see any fishing gear."

"Hell no; I don't fish. Like I said the last time, I'm here to work on my tan and to gawk at the hunks."

He laughs, "Oh, that's right. Judging by your tan for this time of the year, you must come often. It looks great."

"Every Saturday afternoon. I just love the fun atmosphere; as well as the sun," she says.

"What about the hunks? Found any yet?" he teases.

"Not today; until just now, that is," she answers in her natural uncontrollable flirting way. "What are you doing here, Mr. Detective? Investigating?"

He finds himself enchanted by her penetrating green eyes but does manage to say, with a stutter, "I; I'm here with my girlfriend. That's her over there. Come on, I'll introduce you."

125

As they walk toward Julie, Sunshine whispers, "She's beautiful!"

"There are a lot of beautiful girls on this pier today," he says softly so that only Sunshine hears him. "Julie, I want you to meet Susan Peters, better known as Sunshine; Miss Peters, this is Julie."

Sunshine offers her hand and says, "Hello Julie; it's a pleasure to meet you. I met your handsome boyfriend right here, on the day of the incident with that little girl. Wasn't that awful?"

Steven grimaces as he listens to Sunshine's innocent comment.

"Hello, Ms. Peters," she says abruptly and with a forced grin. Steven, can we go now? I've seen enough."

"Sure Baby," he answers as Julie hurriedly turns away. He appears stunned as he nods an embarrassed good-bye to Sunshine.

They walk the length of the pier without a word being said until, "That was rather rude don't you think? Why did you act like that?" he asks as they approach the car.

"I wasn't aware that I was acting one way or the other. I just wanted to get off that damn pier."

+ + + +

They kiss each other lightly as Steven sees her to her apartment door. He says as he leaves, "I guess today's excursion didn't cure you of your demons. I'm sorry about that."

"I don't want to talk about it," she says closing the door behind her.

126

He shakes his head in frustration, as well as aggravation, as he slowly walks to the elevator. After forcibly punching the call button, he stands motionless staring at the stainless steel doors, listening to the rumble that signals its approach.

CHAPTER THIRTY-SIX

Four Weeks After The Incident
Sunday, April 21, 2013 at 11:00 AM

"Abby, this is Rick. He's that sweet good-looking man I have been telling you about."

Rick bends down and takes Abby's hand and says, "Wow! You are beautiful! Your mother said you were gorgeous and cute as a shiny button and she was right. I'm Rick. Welcome to my home."

"Mommy, are we going to live here?"

"Yes, Baby; me, you, and Rick are going to be together here in Rick's home; in Navarre."

"Not Justin?"

"No Baby, not Justin; just us three. . . . What do you think?"

"Nice. Can I look around?"

"Sure, Abby," Rick says. "Your special bedroom is the one at the end of the hall. And go look at the back yard. There's lots of room for you to run."

+ + + +

After a long day of moving and rearranging furniture, Rick says to Maggie, "That's it's. Everything is in place. I'm exhausted. . . . Now, Baby, come here and sit by me on the couch. I've waited for a month to put my arms around you again and I'm not going to wait any longer."

"Abby was worn out too. She just loves her new room. She passed out as soon as she lied down and closed her eyes," Maggie adds. "I'm just going to open the wine and I'll be right there."

"I can wait for that," he says softly as he leans his head back, kicks off his boots, places a small throw pillow on the coffee table, stretches out his long legs, and placing his heals on the pillow. Maggie joins him as she asks, "What's with the pillow?"

"I have very tender feet; probably the most sensitive known to man."

A small smile crosses her face as she joins him. They sit in silence, totally relaxed, occasionally sipping on the wine.

"Take me to your bed, Rick," she whispers.

"I'll take you to our bed," he says as he lifts and carries her to their room.

+ + + +

Rick lies her down on the bed without pulling down the covers. He leans over her, supporting himself on his two arms, and kisses her long and hard. He stands and asks, "Would you like to freshen up or shower? I for one feel a little grimy after today."

"No, but I'd love a bubble bath. Would you like to join me?" she asks with a broad teasing grin.

"Does a pelican eat fish? You run the hot water and I'll go get the soap from the kitchen. It's all I have," he says excitedly.

"I've brought some bath soap from my place. It makes big beautiful scented bubbles."

"Scented too, huh? Yippy!" he teases.

"I've missed you so much," they each express as they embrace and kiss repeatedly while the water churns the soap.

After a few minutes Rick tests the temperature and says, "It's perfect!"

"Great; get in!"

"Oh, no you don't! This time you go first," he insists.

Remembering the first day on the boat she laughs and begins to slowly strip off her clothes. He steps back and watches her leisurely remove one item after another then neatly fold and place it on a small table beside the bubble filled tub. He stares at her in silence; not making any effort to remove anything of his. She shakes her head allowing her bound hair to fall haphazardly across her shoulders and down her back. After shedding her bra and gently stepping out of her panties, she purposely pauses a second allowing him time to fully admire her flawless body. She grins to herself knowing that he is watching closely as she carefully steps in with one foot and feels for the hot water. Finding it satisfactory, she slowly settles into the bubbles while saying with a whisper, "Okay big boy; my turn to watch."

He laughs and rapidly strips off everything and practically jumps in causing the bubbles as well as several gallons of water to spill across the floor. They embrace for a second, stand, hurriedly step out of the tub, run covered with those beautiful scented bubbles, and dive onto the bed.

CHAPTER THIRTY-SEVEN

Five Weeks After The Incident
Friday, April 26, 2013 at 6:00 PM

The text message from Julie reads, 'Dear Steven, I resigned from my coroner's job today, effective immediately. I am already on the road to Colorado. You have been a sweet and good friend. Love, Julie.

He tosses the phone onto his sofa and stares at nothing.

CHAPTER THIRTY-EIGHT

Five Weeks After The Incident
Saturday, April 27, 2013 at 3:00 PM

Steven walks with a purpose to the end of the pier. He sees Sunshine as he had hoped and approaches without her noticing. He asks without hesitation, "Would you have dinner with me tonight?"

Startled, she looks over her shoulder and also without dithering, answers, "Of course."

"Great! I can pick you up if you give me your address. I would like to go to the Ocean Club if that's alright with you.

"I'll meet you there. Would seven be okay?"

"Seven will be fine," he answers. He takes a few steps to leave but pauses and returns to her. He places his hands on either side of her face and kisses her gently. He straightens up and says, "I hope you didn't mind that. I had to see something. I had to see how it felt."

"And?"

"It was thrilling. It was as I had hoped. . . . Actually it was more; quite a bit more."

She pulls his face down by his shirt collar and returns the kiss. "What do you see and feel now, Detective?" she asks.

"I'll see you at seven," he laughs and calls out over his shoulder as he departs.

+ + + +

Glancing around the restaurant, Sunshine says, "Wow, Detective, this is a fancy place. Are you sure you can afford it? I must warn you that I can really shove it down the old goosel."

"Goosel! . . . What the hell is a goosel?

"You know; your goosel!" she answers as she begins a slight giggle while looking into his eyes. She can sense that this might be fun.

"No, I don't know. Where is it; did you bring it with you?" he asks seriously confused as Sunshine breaks out into a full belly laugh.

"Yes, yes, I brought it with me," she laughs as she stares at his dumbfounded expression.

"Well, . . . show it to me!"

"Oh, Detective. You have got to stop with the one-liners. I can't laugh any more, my sides are killing me."

As his expression gradually turns to a grin, he says, "Please let me in on the joke."

"Your gullet; your craw! Hasn't your mama ever said to you after you choke on something, 'it must have gone down the wrong goosel?'"

"There's more than one?" he asks with a serious face.

"Oh, goodness; I can't take it; my sides; my aching sides," she manages to say between outburst of laughter. Slowly regaining her composure, she continues, "Where do you come from? Everybody I associate with knows about the goosel and how sensitive it is to the choke."

"I was born up north, in North Dakota. My family moved down here when I was a kid to get out of the cold."

"Oh, that explains it. My kin are mainly from North Carolina. I grew up eating butter beans, collards, okra, sweet corn on the cob, and pan fried chicken. Ninety-nine point nine percent never touched my goosel; it all just slid on pass. . . . Oh, look; our table's ready."

+ + + +

"That was a fantastic dinner. Thank you Detective."

He tips his glass of wine to her and says, "You're welcome, but will you please stop calling me Detective?"

"Of course. What would you prefer? How about good-looking, or handsome, or maybe even hunk?"

"You are a serious nut. How about Steven or Steve?"

"Okay, I can do that," she says and then continues, "It's early; what's the plan?"

"Oh, I don't know. I just thought we would hang out together awhile; go down to the beach . . . or to my apartment; I'd like to show you something."

"Whoa. You slipped that one in there pretty easily," she says with an obvious disappointed expression on her face. She slides the chair back and begins to stand as she continues to say, "I was hoping that you thought more of me than that; that I would be good catch for a one-night stand. I seriously didn't think you were that sort of guy."

"Oh my God! I'm sorry. I didn't mean that. It came out all wrong. I'm not that kind of guy. I'm not. I'm so sorry. I think you're fantastic, you're marvelous. It just came out because I wanted to show you something that I am very proud of; something I love. I keep it a secret from most of my friends. They'll think I'm nuts for having one and I know they will constantly tease me. I wanted to share it with you because I consider you special. I haven't known you for very long but I really like you. That's all. I just wanted you to see it. I'm sorry. We can go if you like but I really wish you would sit back down. I'll tell you."

Sunshine slowly pulls her chair back up to the table and says, "Okay Steve, Steven, Detective; whatever you call yourself, let's hear it."

He leans in and says softly, "I have a shih pooh."

"Pardon me!"

"I have a shih pooh," he repeats.

"Well go ahead! You had better ask the waiter because I don't have any idea where the men's room is located."

With a chuckle, he explains, "It's a little dog; a cross between a shih tzu and a miniature poodle. Her name is Calico, because of all her colors. She's pregnant; expecting two pups within a couple of weeks."

"I would expect a shih pooh to drop offspring daily," Sunshine says with a teasing grin. "Why wouldn't you let your friends know? It's just a dog."

"Because it's a tiny dog. I'm supposed to be a tough guy; have a tough guy image; own a German Shepherd or a pit bull. Calico weighs about four pounds and can fit in my hand. I would never hear the end of the teasing down at the station."

"Well, I think it's sweet and I think you're sweet. I'm sorry I doubted you and questioned your intentions."

"No apology needed. . . . So, do you want to go meet her?"

"Of course. . . . I had a cat once. It couldn't stand me. All it wanted was for me to feed it and keep its litter box clean. I learned that the less you feed a cat the fewer times you have to clean out the box. The darn thing finally moved in with the neighbors."

"You're a real mess, Sunshine," he laughs.

"I've been told that before. . . . You do realize that I am not a prude, don't you Steven?"

"I was hoping that was the case."

CHAPTER THIRTY-NINE

Four Months After The Incident
Friday, July 12, 2013 at 6:00 PM

Rick Rubio enters his home shouting, "Maggie! Maggie! I have some unbelievable news!" He runs from room to room but can't find her. He sees Abby and asks her, "Where's your Mommy. I have some good news."

"She's in the back yard; in the garden. She's all dirty."

Running through the back screen door he shouts, "My boss wants to sell me the shop; boat, gear, equipment, everything! Can you believe it?"

"Oh, my; why?" she asks as she pulls off her dirt covered gloves.

"He said he's tired of it. Says it's too much for him. I think he may have some health problems. I don't know. Says he'll even finance it."

"That's fantastic!" Maggie yells. "Not his health problems but the news."

He laughs saying, "He knows that I will eventually open my own and I think he believes he couldn't go it alone."

"Oh, Baby, I'm so happy for you, for us," she again says as she jumps into his outstretched arms. He spins around and around and her legs fly high nearly destroying the tall tomato plants that she had been tending.

"Put me down you crazy man. Let's go inside and get cleaned up. Tonight is a night for us to celebrate!" she exclaims for all to hear.

+ + + +

"Abby, this was a great choice. You picked a great spot. I bet you like pizza almost as much as I do," Rick kids her.

"More!" she shouts with a giggle.

"You've eaten enough Abby. Why don't you take your shoes off and go play in the fun room. We can watch you through those big old windows," Maggie says.

"Okay, Mommy." She looks at Rick and asks, "Is that okay with you, Daddy?"

Rick stares at her and dips his head 'yes' and lightly touches the top of her golden head. That was all he could do. That's the first time she has called him Daddy. Maggie has often told her she could but only if that was what she really wanted. He wipes his eyes as it became obvious that it was exactly what Abby wanted.

.

CHAPTER FORTY
Four Months After The Incident
Monday, July 15, 2013 at 11:00 AM

"Rick, I hate to call you at the shop but I couldn't wait until you got home to tell you that we are having a couple of really good days."

"Oh, yeah, what's up?" he asks.

"I just got off the phone with the state's lawyer. He said that they will be wiring, this coming Friday, one million, five hundred thousand dollars into my bank account."

. . . . "Oh, my; oh, my; oh, my! . . . Really? I can't believe it!" he says as he fights to hold back any outward display of his exuberance, realizing that he's on the shop's phone and there are customers around.

"Believe it! I'm going out this afternoon and scout out condos on the beach," she says.

"Pick out a good one. My only request is that it has a shower built for two."

"That little wish shall be granted, My Love."

"Have to go now. I love ya, Maggie."

+ + + +

That evening, he asks, "Did you find a condo that you liked? Tell me about it if you did."

"I did. It's glorious. Unbelievable views of the Gulf as well as up and down the beach. I put an offer in already."

"Ha, ha; that's my girl! Which one is it and when can I see it? I feel like it's Christmas Eve and can't wait to see what's under the tree," he says.

"The Tower; one floor below the penthouse. It's vacant; we can see it any time. We can move in within a month."

"The Tower! Wow! That's pretty fancy. Let's start packing."

CHAPTER FORTY-ONE

Five Months After The Incident
Saturday, August 24, 2013 at 11:00 AM

"Here and now, before this congregation, would each of you like to offer your solemn vows to each other?" the minister asks.

"We would," answers Sunshine and Steven simultaneously.

"Please proceed."

Steven begins nervously, "Give me your hand and I'll feel what you feel. Give me your eyes and I'll see what you see. Give me your burden and I'll carry what you carry. Give me your joy and I'll be joyful too. You have given me your heart and I'll love and cherish it forever."

Sunshine says, after clearing her throat, "Here is my hand; I feel what you're feeling. Here are my eyes; I see what you're seeing. I accept our burden and we'll carry it together. Take my joy and we'll be joyful together. You have given me your heart and I'll love and cherish it forever."

"By the powers vested in me by the state of Alabama I pronounce you husband and wife. Ladies and gentlemen, please allow me to introduce to you, Mr. Steven Sunshine Acer and Mrs. Susan Sunshine Peters Acer."

Completing their long passionate kiss they turn and bow to the congregation. After only a few minutes of accepting congratulations Steven waves his arms and shouts, "Now clear a path, we're off to the beach!"

"Are you going to carry me over the threshold Detective?"

"Why is it understood that the husband carries the wife across the threshold?"

"Well, it's basically because y'all are generally big strong lugs and us brides are petite weaklings," she explains.

"I don't think that's fair. In today's world we are supposed to be equal. The bride could plan ahead and have a wheel barrel or a grocery cart or even a Radio Flyer red wagon delivered to the door, waiting for the horny couple to arrive. Then the big lug could climb aboard and the petite little wife could just push or pull him over the threshold."

"You're a real piece of work, Detective. Your promise to me, after your proposal, of no sex before marriage has apparently resulted in some sort of fluid backup that has reached all the way to your brain."

"Now that, my lovely new wife, I can agree with."

"What's the name of the condo? Slow down! I want to spot it before you," she excitedly says as she strains to read the name on each tall building they pass.

"The Tower."

"Keep going. Oh, there it is. I see it. Wow! What a place. It's beautiful and right on the beach," she announces.

"Anything for my bride. I like to bring all my new wives here," he jokes.

"Funny; let's hurry."

Waiting for the elevator Steven points and says laughing, "Look, there's a cart."

"Will you please be so kind and kiss my tail, Detective Acer?"

"After I get this dang elevator to cooperate, I plan to do just that, My Dear."

Finally arriving at their floor and carrying her into the condo, he asks, "Okay, I carried you over the threshold. Where do you want me to place you?"

"Place me? Let's see, let me look around a second. Now where would I look the best?" she says playing alone. "What do you think Detective?"

"I can stand you up right here in the middle of the floor. What about that?"

"I guess that's okay," she says.

"Or, I could sit you down on that red seagull and purple dolphin covered sofa."

"That's better," she says.

"Or, I could lie you down on a bed that I am pretty sure I can find somewhere in this fancy place."

"That's the best. I'll look great in bed," she says.

They laugh out loud as he gently places her on a large king sized bed covered with numerous colorful throw pillars. He kisses her and begins to leave the room. "Where are you going?" she asks.

"I was going to leave you alone so that you could get out of that wedding dress and into something more comfortable."

"I was planning on you helping me out of it," she says with a sly grin.

143

He again begins to leave the room. "Good grief, now where are you going?" she asks with a smile but slightly confused .

"I'm going to get the scissors."

They both break out in out-of-control laughter as he dives onto the bed beside her.

+ + + +

"That was unbelievable," she whispers.

"I'm glad you liked it," he calmly says. "I try to please."

She elbows him in his ribs as he laughs at his own teasing. She giggles and kisses his neck as she pulls him over her again.

+ + + +

"What's the plan for the next two weeks, big boy?" she asks as they remain in bed.

"Well tonight and through the day tomorrow I thought we'd stay in bed and practice what we've been doing until we get it right."

"I'll go along with that. What about the day after that and the ones following?" she asks.

"Well, the first thing each day we need to practice. I'm a real stickler for perfection. We'll probably need to work at it in the evenings also."

"No doubt; and in between?"

"I thought we would get in some snorkeling and even a little scuba diving."

"That sounds neat but I know absolutely nothing about diving," she says.

"Me either, so I scheduled beginner classes with a professional diver at a local dive shop. I found it on the internet and checked the place out. They have a great reputation. So what do you think?"

"Count me in, but are you sure you wouldn't like to just stay in bed and practice?" she teases.

"That was a close second."

CHAPTER FORTY-TWO

Five Months After The Incident
Monday, August 26, 2013 at 10:00 AM

"Hello, I'm Steven Acer. Are you Rick? I believe I scheduled scuba classes with you a few weeks back."

"Oh, yeah! Hi, I'm Rick Rubio," he answers as he extends his hand.

"Hi, Rick; this lovely lady tagging along with me is my bride, Susan, or, if you wish, Sunshine."

She pokes her new husband in the ribs as she says, "Nice to meet you, Rick."

"And the same to you, Sunshine. You don't mind if I choose Sunshine do you? That's a lovely name."

"Of course not, that's my name. . . . Have we met before? You look sort of familiar," she asks.

"I don't think so; been around these parts most of my life. Where are you guys from?"

"Gulf Shores; Steven's a detective with the police department. We lived there most of our lives," she proudly says. "As of the moment, I'm a bum."

Laughing, Rick says, "I'm still in the process of getting things set up for y'all. I understood that you wouldn't be here until one."

"That's right; we just wanted to look around. Sort of get the-lay-of-the-land of your shop. Check out the equipment, the gear, stuff like that. We weren't doing anything but hanging around the condo anyway," he says as he continues to lovingly tease Sunshine.

146

Again he takes a shot to the ribs but this time accompanied by a warning stare. He just grins.

+ + + +

"Okay, Baby; let's get going. We've been here too long. I've seen and learned just enough to make me confused. Are you ready to go? We can get an early lunch and get ready to get back here for one o'clock. You can call your friend and ask her how Calico is doing," Steven says.

"That'll work. . . . Thanks, Rick; see you at one," Sunshine shouts as they leave the shop.

"Oh, wait; before you go I want to take our picture together. I do this for all my customers. They like to use it as proof that they really did dive. I might forget later," he says.

"That's a good idea. Can you email or text it to us?" Sunshine asks.

"Sure." The three of them line up in front of the shop as Rick has a junior clerk snap the photo. "See y'all at one," he shouts.

CHAPTER FORTY-THREE

Five Months After The Incident
Friday, August 30, 2013 at 5:30 PM

Arriving back at their condo, Sunshine says, "You know Steven, My Love; we've been taking the lessons for a week now and I believe I'm finally getting the hang of this breathing underwater thing."

"Yeah, I saw that. I'm getting pretty comfortable myself," he says.

"But I still can't get it out of my mind that I have met Rick before. It's beginning to haunt me."

"Well, he's a good looking guy. I'm sure you've looked at a bunch of good looking guys in the past and he probably resembles one of them," he says in an attempt to explain her confusion.

Extended silence from her causes Steven to ask, "What's going on? What's running through that pretty little mind of yours? I can see the wheels turning."

"That's it. You said it. You gave me the clue. I know where I saw him. You're not going to believe this. . . . Oh my God!" she shrieks as she places a hand over her mouth.

"Good Heavens! What's the matter? Why did you cry out like that? You startled me. Are you okay, Baby?" he asks as her actions start to concern him.

"Yes, I'm good. It's just upsetting."

"What the hell are you talking about? Stop with the dramatics! Apparently you've realized how you know him. How? Tell me now. Just calm down and say it."

"He was on the pier."

"What pier? A lot of people visit the piers around here."

"Damnit, Steven; he was on our pier; the Gulf Shores pier. That pier! I saw him there the day that baby was thrown over," she explains as she does begin to calm down.

"Really, I don't remember seeing him. He must have left before I arrived."

"You've got that right," she says even managing to smile at her inside joke.

"I got what right? What did I do that was right? And what the hell are you grinning about?" he asks as her contagious smile begins spreading across his face. He tries but he can't stop it from widening so he gives in and lets it morph into a full blown giggle. She in turn joins him in the unprovoked merriment.

They finally get themselves under control and Steven says, "We haven't been married for even a full week yet and you have already made me act like a crazy person. One minute I'm asking my wife a perfectly legitimate question and the next minute I've lost all self control and I am laughing, for no reason, like a nervous hyena. Now please tell me, with a straight face, are you sure it was Rick?"

"I can't look at you. I'll start giggling again."

"Well, then look away or go into the bedroom and shout out the answer."

"That's a good idea," she says as she hurries out of his sight.

He yells, "Alright let's start over. Are you ready? Are you sure it was Rick on that pier and what was he doing there?"

"I'm ninety percent sure and he was jumping over the rail to save that little girl," she bellows.

Hearing that, he runs into the bedroom and says, "You can't be serious. That's not possible! That poor soul was eaten by sharks. There was blood!"

"I think it's him, Steven. He's clean shaven now and he's cut his long hair but I remember other things; like the way he walks and just the way he carries himself. Heck, I might even have a picture of him on the pier."

"A picture? Why in the world would you have a picture of him?"

"If you remember, I told you I went to the pier quite often because I liked to check out the hunks. I've even got photos of you," she says with a sly grin. "I took them with my cell phone. The subject didn't know he was being photographed."

"I can't dispute that last point if you have my picture from that day. I'd like to see them; of me and of him," he says. Pausing and thinking out loud he continues, "He certainly is a strong swimmer and he is a professional diver. He has access to all sorts of underwater gear, tools, and equipment. He even has use of a good sized boat. If something like this was to be pulled off he would be a perfect candidate. But why; what would be the motive?"

"You're the detective. You figure it out. As for me, I'm going to get naked and request that you join me. I'd like to get in a little practice before dinner."

+ + + +

Wow! Well that surely worked up my appetite," Steven says. "What about you, Darling?"

"I don't believe I have enough energy to lift a fork. Why don't we stay in and eat cheese and crackers. We can wash it down with a bottle of merlot. That should build up our energy; probably enough to allow us to get in more practice before it's time to actually sleep."

"Sunshine, you can come up with the best ideas."

CHAPTER FORTY-FOUR

Five and One Half Months After The Incident
Monday, September 2, 2013 at 1:00 PM

"Hi guys, it seems like y'all were finally getting the hang of it last Friday. You both looked quite comfortable under the water. I don't think y'all will have any trouble when we make our little dive later this week. You'll have a lot of confidence by then and that's really all it takes. And me of course," Rick says and laughs.

"Yeah, we're getting there. Now that we know some of the lingo, can I ask you about some of this equipment you have hanging on your walls?" Steven asks.

"Shoot. What do you want to know?"

Pointing, he asks, "What is that used for; that thing there on the table that looks like a small torpedo?"

"That tows the diver. You just hang on and it takes you where you want to go in a hurry and with little effort from the diver," he explains.

"I see; what about this rather odd looking scuba pact?"

"That's called a rebreather. You reuse your own air. That's the coming thing in diving. It doesn't release any bubbles. I think the military came up with it, I guess to sneak up on the bad guys," he laughs.

"And that little tube that you have in your display case?" he points.

"That's extra air. That's really handy in emergencies. It's small and easy to carry."

"Of course you have the wetsuits, goggles, mask, swim fins; everything anyone would need to be a diver."

"That's what we try to be around here; your one stop dive shop," he says but this time without a smile. "Ya'll go get into your gear. I want to check on the long term weather forecast and then I'll be right there."

It's true, he does want to check on the weather but he also wants some time to clear his head. He's confused with the number of questions and the tone Steven used to ask them. Why ask all that now, all of a sudden? He also wanders why Sunshine said nothing the whole time but just seemed to stare at him; measuring or studying him. She did ask him again at the end of last week if he was sure they had never met. He wonders if that ties in with the questions.

"The weather looks good through the week. Just a slightly higher chance of thunderstorm toward the end but we should be good to go on Friday morning as scheduled."

"Sounds great, Rick. Let's get down to work!"

CHAPTER FORTY-FIVE

Five and One Half Months After The Incident
Wednesday, September 4, 2013 at 10:00 AM

"It sure is nice to get a break from those lessons. They were beginning to wear me out," Sunshine says.

"That's why Rick told us he'll see us Friday morning; gives us a few days to get some of our strength and stamina back. . . . Changing the subject, were you ever able to locate those pictures we were talking about?"

"Oh, yeah, I sure did," she answers as she tosses him the phone. "I rearranged them so that they are the last ones that pop up. Just press 'photo' and you'll see."

After thumbing through the pictures, he says, "Well, they are not exactly close-ups. I recognize me but I can't tell if that's Rick or not. Not with the cap, long hair hanging out of it, and a lot of facial hair. I know my photo was taken on that day but none of them has us in it together. The photos of the 'maybe Rick' could have been taken on any day. Does this phone record the dates?"

"I don't think so. It's a pretty old phone," she answers.

Handing her the phone he says, "There's no way to identify who that person is. Sorry, Baby."

"Oh, well. . . . Look, I'm going to walk down to the beach, lie out a while, and work on my tan. Would you like to join me?" she asks.

"No thanks. I think I'll just stay up here in the cool and try to finish my novel before we have to return home. You go ahead."

+ + + +

"Welcome back, Baby. I thought that you would be down there a couple of hours."

"I was down there long enough. I have some news," she says.

"News; what sort of news? I'm really not interested in any local gossip? Can you tell me later? I want to finish this chapter."

"Put the book down," she orders.

"Pardon me!" He looks up at her and sees she has a grin spread from ear to ear. "Oh, no! We're not going to go through this again. Spell it out. Turn around if you have to but please just say what you want to say."

"I met Abby and her mother."

"That's nice. Who the heck is Abby?"

"You're not going to believe it?"

"Oh my God! Please Mrs. Susan Sunshine Peters Acer, don't do this to me again!" he begs.

"She is the little girl that was thrown off the pier into the Gulf of Mexico," she says.

"Did she wash up on the beach?" he asks.

"It's not funny. Abigail James is her name and her mother is Margaret James They own a condo here in the Towers," she states.

"Owns a condo? Did you say 'owns?' . . . A condo here in this fancy place?" he asks as his detective juices start flowing.

"Yes. And guess what actually did wash up on the beach; came right out of the surf as I was sitting there talking to Maggie. Margaret said I could call her Maggie," she says with that sly grin.

"Please, Sunshine; I'm begging you. Spit it out!"

"You really are going to be floored by this."

"Please!"

"It seems that our diving instructor also took the day off."

"No way!"

"Came bounding out of the sea all decked out in his weenie bikini looking like Poseidon himself. If he had a trident, I would have immediately started looking around for Zeus. I must say that that skimpy suit was working overtime holding everything in its proper place. He joined us and we had just a fine old time. Seems like they all live together as one big happy family. Allow me to digress a moment; they are amazing together. There is really a whole lot of obvious love going back and forth between them. And that little girl calls him Daddy and it's easy to see he worships her, as well as her mommy. They are quite a family."

Steven stood up while Sunshine was talking and was now pacing slowly back and forth from the couch to the balcony door.

Sunshine could see he was weighing things. "What do you think," she asks.

"I think we've found the motive."

"Really; what is it?"

"Money! The motive is money; insurance money."

CHAPTER FORTY-SIX

Five and One Half Months After The Incident
Wednesday, September 4, 2013 at 12:30 PM

"Hi, Steven. What the hell are you doing calling into the office? I thought that you were still on your honeymoon. Getting tired of that stuff already?"

"No, not really; we're still trying to work out the kinks," he answers with a laugh in his voice.

"Well then, you must be checking up on your cute, tiny, little puppy."

"How did you know about her?" Steven asks with a surprised tone.

"This is a small community my friend. I bought one of those for my Brutus once; he loved it but wouldn't eat his dry food for a week."

"Funny," Steven says with an irritated tone.

"Sorry Boss; just having a little fun. What's up?"

"I need you to look into something for me. Remember that thing on the pier a few months back? I want you to pull that file and let me know if anything has developed on it since then. I want to know what sort of details came out at the trial; what all that idiot said; things like that. Then I need you to look into a Richard Rubio of Navarre. He works at the Dive Shop. Also, I'd like a little background on the baby's mother, Margaret James. Can you handle that for me?" Steven asks.

"Not a problem. When do you need it? If you can believe it, things have been sort of slow so I can get right on it."

"This afternoon if you can get it but no later than tomorrow before noon," Steven answers.

"I'll do it. Now, go back to bed."

"Will do," he says smiling as he hangs up the phone and immediately calls out, "Sunshine!"

"Yes! . . . I'm in the kitchen."

"The guys at the office told me go back to bed."

"Was it an order from the main man?"

"I believe it was."

"Well, let me put this big ripe banana back where it belongs and I'll be right in; or more appropriately, you'll be right in."

He laughs and says, "You are so nasty!"

"I know, and you love it!"

"You've got that right."

CHAPTER FORTY-SEVEN

Five and One Half Months After The Incident
Wednesday, September 4, 2013 at 1:00 PM

"Abby's down for her nap. Can I interest you in a quickie?" Maggie asks.

"Of course, but we have to talk about something first."

"What? What's on your mind? You haven't said two words since we came up."

"That girl you met down on the beach, Sunshine; she's married to a police detective from Gulf Shores."

"Oh, no," she interrupts.

"They've been taking scuba lessons from me for the last week and a half. Lately I've been getting these weir vibes from them. I think they are suspicious of something."

"What; suspicious of what? What makes you say that?" she asks feeling her heart rate climb.

"Her husband, Steven, has started asking a bunch of questions and Sunshine swears she has seen me before," he explains.

"Do you recognize her?"

"No; I don't ever remember seeing her. Never. . . . It's not her I'm worried about, it's him."

"Oh my God! Do you think he knows something?"

"I'm not sure."

"This can't be happening. What are we going to do? Should we run? I'm scared. Oh my God!" she repeats as her nerves begin to effect her thinking.

"No, of course not. I'll think of something. . . . We need more information. Can you Google the incident on the pier? It was a big story for the first couple of days. Pull up some of the articles. Maybe it can tell us something."

"You think this could be about Abby and the pier?" she asks as her hand begins to shake.

"If it's not, then we have nothing to fear. If we find out that it is, I make a promise to you that we will all be okay. I'll figure something out. Please try to calm down. I need you to keep a level head," he softly says as he kisses her forehead. "Now, let's see what's on Google."

Sunshine is silent as she scans several articles. Then she gasps, lowers her head into her hands, and cries. Rick bends down, looks over her shoulder, and reads *Detective Steven Acer will head up the investigation.*

"Rick, what are we going to do? We could go to jail. And what about Abby? My sweet little Abby; what will happen to her?" she manages to say between sobs.

"I don't know. I'll do something. I'm scheduled to take them on their first dive Friday morning. If we're not arrested by then, it's probably because they don't have any proof or at the worst, not enough proof. Then I can talk to them; find out what if anything they have. Then I'll go from there."

"What do you mean, you'll go from there?" she asks frightened at what he might say.

"If they have the proof, I'll react one way. If they don't, I'll react another way. That's all I'm saying."

"Rick. . . . Promise me you will not resort to violence. Promise me you won't hurt these people. No matter what might ultimately happen to us, promise me."

He knows what Maggie is telling him. She's saying not to take these people out into the Gulf of Mexico and have an accident; not to fake a diving mishap of some sort. It hasn't even crossed his mind but he is realizing now that it's something that maybe he should not completely discard. He knows that he's not the kind of person who would go to those extremes but on the other hand he will do whatever it takes to keep him and Maggie and Abby together. He has to find out what they know, or think they know, and he won't have that answer until Friday morning. Then he'll decide what to do.

"Rick, stop staring out of the window! Promise me!" she demands.

"I promise. . . ." He kisses her forehead, takes her hand, and says, "Let's go work on that quickie."

CHAPTER FORTY-EIGHT

Five and One Half Months After The Incident
Friday, September 6, 2013 at 9:00 AM

"Hi, guys! Right on time. I've already loaded the boat with the gear. Also brought along a few snacks in case you want to munch on something. I'm sure that your stomachs are a bit nervous. It seems to help me. We have a beautiful day, but thunderstorms can pop up at anytime. So, let's get moving. Did you bring an extra bag; change of clothes or something, maybe some sunscreen? I'll go get it you did. Come aboard," Rick rattles on nervously.

He smiles at Sunshine as he offers his hand to assist her stepping on board. She doesn't say anything but manages a rather obviously forced grin. At least he interprets is as forced. The fact that they have shown up alone, and not accompanied by arresting police officers, lifts his spirits ever so slightly.

"Alright Steven; your turn," he says.

"I'd like to talk to you for a second first. Can you step out of the boat and come up here?"

"Sure, what's up? Got some butterflies?" he asks fully knowing what's up.

"I understand Sunshine met Margaret James and her daughter Abigail down on the beach the day before yesterday. I also understand that you are living with them in her condo."

"That's right," Rick calmly says.

"And, I'm sure that you are aware that little Abby was thrown off of the Gulf Pier back in March and that she was rescued by an unknown hero whose body was never recovered."

"Of course! What are you getting at, Steven? I heard that the poor fellow was attached by sharks."

"I have reason to believe that that poor fellow is you. I also have reason to believe that you and Ms. James conspired to stage the event in order to defraud the state and receive an insurance reward as well as to get a Mr. Justin Webb out of Ms. James life."

Rick, trying his best to control his nervousness as he prepares himself to ask the next question, says, "Steven, those are pretty serious allegations. Do you have any proof?"

"You bet your wetsuit they're serious allegations. If it's found to be true, you and Ms. James are facing long term jail time. To answer your question, no I don't have any concrete proof but I do have circumstantial proof. I have a witness who says you were there, I have a fuzzy picture of the person which may or may not be you, and I have knowledge of your budding relationship at UWF with Ms. James, probably starting in January or February. I also have the fact that you have detail knowledge and access to equipment that would allow you to pull off this fraud."

Rick realizes that Steven, in fact, has nothing; he can't prove a thing unless some additional evidence surfaces. Now that his spirits are rising he says, "Doesn't sound like you have much, Steven. Under the circumstances, do y'all still want to dive?"

"I'm still looking and I have my people digging also. We'll find more. And yes, we still want to make the trip. Sunshine has her heart set on it. I know that you won't try anything stupid when we're out there on the ocean. I am a trained police officer and am fully capable of protecting myself under any conditions. Do you understand what I'm saying?"

"Let's get aboard and head out," Rick says without answering.

+ + + +

Around fifteen minutes after pulling away from the dock, Rick asks Steven to take over the helm for a second as he needs to visit the head. Out of sight he quickly sends a text message to Maggie that says, *No evidence. All will be fine.* He knows she has been anxious and has been waiting to hear from him.

CHAPTER FORTY-NINE

Five and One Half Months After The Incident
Friday, September 6, 2013 at 10:30 AM

Rick announces, "Okay, we're about fifteen miles out and it looks like we're over the spot. See that blip there?" he says pointing to a small area on the display screen as they look over his shoulder. "That's a group of old World War II army tanks. There're several groups around this general spot. They're in fifty and sixty feet of water; well within y'all diving range. Why I like to come here, especially with beginner divers like yourselves, is because it's shallow enough to anchor the boat which allows me to join you in the first dive. I can keep an eye on you and help if there's an emergency of some sort. There won't be today; y'all are pretty good." Neither Steven nor Sunshine comment.

"Okay, let's get the gear on," Rick orders as he claps his hands. "There's a cumulonimbus cloud building north but it looks as if it's heading out to sea."

Sunshine asks, "What kind of cloud? What does that mean? Is it something to worry about?"

"It's a storm cloud, Baby; it's drifting away. No reason to be concerned," Steven explains.

"Alright, everybody looks good. Who wants to go first? Just stand on the edge of the swim platform; you can see it's only two or three inches above the water. Place one hand over your mask so it doesn't come off when you hit the water and turn around so that you're facing the

165

boat. After that, all you need to do is fall back; the pack hits the water first."

A wary Steven lifts his mask and says, "Rick, you go first."

Rick looks at him and just shakes his head.

CHAPTER FIFTY

Five and One Half Months After The Incident
Friday, September 6, 2013 at 10:40 AM

Sunshine is the last one to enter the water. After the initial noise of her splash, complete and total silence engulfs her. The only sounds that she can hear are those made by her escaping breath and her pounding heart. Obtaining her bearings she sees that she is looking up at the bottom of the boat so she rolls over and stares down into a new world. Amazing, unbelievable, fantastic, miraculous are but a few of the adjectives that come to her mind. She feels that even those do not do justice to what she is viewing. The bright golden color of the sunlit air above is suddenly transformed to nearly transparent emerald green, sometimes blue, seawater below. She is looking at a new world and she is thrilled. She allows herself to be suspended for several minutes before beginning to descend. She sees Steven and Rick several feet below her and she easily guides down to their level. They all halt and hover just a few feet above what she assumes is one of those tanks that Rick mentioned earlier. It's completely covered with years of sea growth including barnacles, long flowing seaweed, and something that looks like a cluster of oysters. She moves in slowly and extends her hand in an effort to pass it back and forth through the seaweed. Rick, alongside, taps her arm and signals 'no' by waving his finger. She nods okay as she remembers the 'look but don't touch' rule.

Pulling back slightly, she nudges Steven and points toward the open water. A school of red snapper of all sizes lazily swim toward the crusted tank and begin circling. The fish ignore her as well as the other two divers as they go about the business of nosing into the seaweed in an obvious search for a meal. Their hunt results in multiple small fish scurrying from their hoped for place of safety. Sunshine just hovers and marvels at the brilliant incandescent blues and bright yellow colors of these escaping little fish. Glancing down she sees a large blue crab dash out of its crevice and grab a wounded victim of the snapper's hunt. Just as quickly, it returns to its notch that it had hollowed out beneath the tank's track. She says to herself that she would like to have that big fellow, along with several ears of corn-on-the-cob and a mess of new potatoes, boiling in spicy seasoned water in a pot on her stove. They swim over to a second tank and witness a school of large, twenty to thirty pound, golden colored redfish, with their distinctive black dots near their tail, flash by. She decides to get a closer look at the huge crusted gun barrel on this tank. Several bright yellow, oval shaped little fish, about four inches in length, slowly venture out of the muzzle but retreat rapidly when they spot her. She swims around to get a better view of these fascinating and beautiful little fish but abruptly halts her advance when she notices a lionfish lurking beneath the turret. Rick warned them about this unbelievable beautiful, but venomous creature. It's red and white stripes, its long pectoral fins, and its row of needles that serve as a dorsal fin, are a marvel to behold. Rick said it will sting a human and the person will indeed get sick.

Wanting to show her diving mates the discovery, she looks over just in time to see Rick tap his wrist watch and point toward the surface. She hates to leave what she considers a paradise but knows that the air is probably getting short. It seems as if only a few minutes have passed but logically she knows it's been longer.

+ + + +

Rick is the first to notice the problem. He checks the GPS readings on his watch and sees that they are where they should be. Looking up, he sees that the boat is not. He also notices that the waters around them have suddenly turned much darker. He instantly identifies what is going on; a thunderstorm is in progress and the boat's anchor has broken free of the sandy bottom. He notices Steven and Sunshine's nervous movements and signals with both hands to settle down, be steady. A few seconds later he motions for them to follow him up. They ascend slowly until they reach and hover approximately six feet below the troughs of the passing waves. Judging the depth of each trough, Rick knows that the waves rolling by above are, at the moment, three or four footers. Rick also is reasonably confident that the storm is one of those quick developing, quick passing summer storms. As it moves on, the choppy seas above should die down. He checks his watch again after which he signals to Steven and Sunshine by tapping his air hose and holding up five fingers. They indicate by nodding their heads 'yes' that they understand and that they will run out of precious air in five minutes.

Rick spends the five minutes planning his next moves. He's realistic and knows that the three of them are in trouble. And, depending on how far the boat has drifted, it could be big trouble. For a brief moment, the thought that a solution to his and Maggie's potential problems with the law has fallen into his lap. He knows that he is a strong swimmer and that they are at best average. Without flotation, which they do not have, he knows that there is a limit to the time that they will be able to tread water; four maybe six hours at the most. He could stay afloat for at least twenty-four hours. He erases the thought from his mind as quickly as it entered.

As the minutes tick down they all notice that the sea in brightening and the wave turbulence seems to be diminishing; all good signs that the storm has indeed moved away. Rick signals it's time to go up. He darts to the surface and instantly shoves his mask up to his forehead, unsnaps the scuba gear strap that crosses his chest and slides is off his shoulders letting it sink. Steven and Sunshine follow his lead. He shouts, "Keep your mask and your fins. Get rid of anything with weight to it; tee shirts, pants, gloves as well. Let it all go. You two stay together."

Rick spends around trying to locate the boat. The first attempt yields nothing. He locates it on the second try. It's much further than he had hoped. He knows it's nearly impossible to estimate distance over open water but he guesses it is at least four to five hundred yards away; five football fields. The wind has died down but the current seems to be moving in the direction of the boat. That's bad. If the anchor hasn't reset itself the boat will continue to move away. He has to act and he has to act now. He yells to his students, "Keep your mask down to protect your eyes and to keep water out of your nose. Use as little energy as possible to keep your head above water; slow kicks and minimum arm movement; use your hands. He demonstrates as he says, "I have to go get the boat. It may keep drifting away. It's our only chance. Any fishermen who may have been around ran to avoid the storm. I can make it there, but it might take a while." Steven and Sunshine nod that they understand.

Rick reaches down and slips off his ankle knife. He hands it to Steven and shouts, "Keep this where you can get at it quickly. Use short straight jabs to the body of any menacing fish. There may be sharks around." Steven takes it without comment.

Rick lowers his mask and begins swimming. After a few freestyle strokes he stops, lifts his mask, and looking straight at Steven, yells "I will be back! . . . I will be back! . . . Take care of your bride!" Steven doesn't acknowledge or display any reaction. Sunshine nods that she understands. Rick begins swimming again.

Steven and Sunshine stare at each other but say nothing as they work to keep afloat. Steven can't help but think and ask himself . . . how did I get us into this mess? Here we are, bobbing up and down fifteen miles out into the Gulf of Mexico, with our lives in the hands of a man who knows I want to put him and his girlfriend in jail for twenty years, plus take a beautiful little girl, who they each clearly love, and put her under the custody of the state.

I'm not even sure what I would do under his circumstances.

CHAPTER FIFTY-ONE

Five and One Half Months After The Incident
Friday, September 6, 2013 at 2:30 PM

Rick sees that he made good progress but estimates that he has a good one hundred yards yet to go. Glancing at his watch he sees it's been over two hours since he started swimming. He's pretty confident that Steven and Sunshine are okay but too much longer, he knows, will be a problem for them. He must pick up the pace. He's thankful it's the summer and the water is nearly as warm as a child's bathwater. Seventy-five yards away he suddenly feels something bump and then pull on one of his fins. He turns; it's a shark. Not a huge shark, five to five and a half feet, but one that can take a sizable chunk out of anything it wants. Thinking . . . oh, no, not again. My more rapid swimming must have attracted this fellow. I don't have time to play around with you buddy. You just have to go on and do your thing or not. I'll try to elude you as much as I can but I'm going to keep swimming.

Ten yards from the swim platform he feels the teeth sink into his right ankle. He suppresses a scream as he attempts to jerk his leg from the shark's powerful jaws. It relaxes its grip only slightly but enough for Rick to free his foot, even though its razor like teeth slice down the top of the foot all the way to his toes. A second bite clamps down on the fin. It whips its head side to side and rips it off Rick's bleeding foot. He grimaces in pain as the shark munches on the fin long enough for Rick to reach the swim platform. He frantically pulls himself on and draws in his legs to get them out of harm's way. He watches as the shark follows the thick trail of blood right to the edge of the platform. From his knees he forcibly knocks open the splash gate and falls, spread eagle and totally exhausted, onto the wide deck.

For several minutes he doesn't move as he regains his strength. He knows the first thing he must do is weigh anchor and crank the motors. He can wrap the foot as he searches for Steven and Sunshine. If it's still bleeding, they can take care of that task during the return trip.

Nearly twenty minutes pass before he locates them and estimates that they are about fifty yards away. He's relieved to see two heads but not pleased to see that they are acting as if they are in real distress. He doesn't understand the abrupt movements they seem to be making. He opens the throttle full ahead and only eases it back to idle when he is nearly on top of them. The boat drifts alongside and they struggle to reach the safety of the swim platform as Rick tosses over two life rings. Out of the corner of his eye he sees the reason for their distress; another shark. This time it's a big one; a nine footer, and it's the fierce bull shark. He's close enough to see, by the slashes on the shark's hide, that Steven has been using the knife but to no avail. He sees the shark circle and knows it's going to come in for another attack. They won't be able to reach the platform before it reaches them. He yells "Swim! Swim!" as he opens one of the storage cabinets and frantically tosses gear onto the deck until he locates and pulls out a four foot long spear gun. He quickly grabs and pulls the three rubbers back and secures them in their slots cut into the spear's stainless steel shaft. The shark approaches Sunshine's midsection as Rick steadies the gun with two hands and squeezes the trigger. The spear, with its razor sharp arrow head, flies over her back and into the broad head of the shark. One quick violent reaction accompanied by a huge explosion of water and then nothing. Rick watches as the shark slowly rolls over and begins sinking head first, due to the weight of the spear, toward the bottom. Two small sharks follow its blood trail down. He hops to the rear of the boat and helps Sunshine and Steven aboard.

"Thanks, Rick," is all that Steven says. Sunshine just sobs.

CHAPTER FIFTY-TWO

Eight Months After The Incident
Friday, November 15, 2013 at 8:00 AM

"Morning, Steven. Get yourself a cup of coffee and come over here and read this article. I think that you will find it quite interesting," says one of several fellow police officers who are standing and bending over a central work table. Another says, "Come see this Steve."

"Well, a good morning to y'all too. What's going on? Can't you give me a chance to take my coat off?" he asks as he walks up to his desk. "What article? What are y'all crowing about?"

"It's an article in our local paper; the one that comes out monthly. We just got it."

"Oh, crap guys! What's it about? I've got plenty to do this morning. Unlike y'all, I don't have time to read newspapers."

"Just get your ass over here and read this! Then tell me you have too much to do," insists the officers. "It's an interview with a little kid who went through a scary experience with his dad. The author or journalist, whatever he calls himself, wrote it in the form of a story being told by the kid on the day it happened. It's neat and we believe you'll find the ending quite interesting. Come on over here and look at this, damnit!"

"Alright. Alright. Move over and let me see what all the hubbub is about!"

The officers step aside and Steven reads:

A BOY'S DAY

DAD FINALLY AGREES AND WE'RE GOING TO TAKE THAT OLD WOODEN SKIFF OUT ON PERDIDO BAY LATER THIS AFTERNOON. I'VE WANTED TO TRY OUT MY NEW SPINNING REEL EVER SINCE HE GAVE IT TO ME LAST MONTH FOR MY BIRTHDAY. OUR BOAT IS ONLY A FOURTEEN FOOT FLAT BUT DAD SAYS IT TAKES THE WAVES WELL BECAUSE IT'S HEAVY. HE REALLY DOESN'T LIKE GOING OUT TOO FAR. BUT HE WANTS TO KEEP HIS PROMISE TO ME; THAT I WILL CATCH THE BIGGEST TROUT IN THE LAKE.

HE'S ALWAYS TALKING ABOUT HOW FAST THE THUNDERSTORMS CAN COME UP IN SEPTEMBER. HE WORRIES BECAUSE IT CAN GET VERY ROUGH VERY FAST. BUT HE SAID TODAY'S WEATHER FORECAST LOOKS GREAT, SO TODAY IS THE DAY.

WE PUT IN AT THE BOAT LAUNCH THAT'S NEXT TO THE COVERED BOAT SLIPS. IT'S DOWN AT THE END OF AN OLD NARROW SINGLE LANE ROAD. DAD CRANKS THE MOTOR AND WE'RE OFF TO LAND THAT TROPHY SPECK.

IT'S HOT. WE CAN'T STOP AND FISH FOR VERY LONG BECAUSE OF THE BLAZING SUN. IT HELPS WHEN THE CLOUDS FINALLY COME OVER AND THE BREEZE STARTS PICKING UP FROM THE SOUTHEAST. WE MOTOR AROUND LOOKING FOR AN OLD DREDGED HOLE WHERE THE REALLY BIG FISH HANG OUT. DAD SAYS THEY LIKE IT NEAR THE BOTTOM BECAUSE THE WATER IS COOL WAY DOWN DEEP.

DAD SAYS IT'S STARTING TO SPRINKLE AND WE WILL HAVE TO HEAD BACK TO THE LAUNCH. HE POINTS TO AN EXPANDING BLACK THUNDERHEAD TO THE NORTH, BEYOND THE LAUNCH. WE STOW OUR GEAR AS BEST WE CAN. ALL THIS GEAR IN THIS LITTLE BOAT AND IT REALLY GETS CROWDED AROUND MY FEET.

IT SEEMS LIKE WE WENT OUT FURTHER THAN USUAL. I CAN BARELY SEE THE DULL GRAY METAL ROOF OF THE BUILDING THAT COVERS THE SLIPS.

DAD GRUNTS AS HE PULLS THE STARTER ROPE OF THE TWELVE HORSEPOWER MOTOR. HE SMILES AT ME AS IT SPITS, SPUTTERS, BUT IT DOES START.

THE OLD FLAT BOTTOM ON THIS BOAT IS REALLY TAKING A POUNDING FROM THE SHORT, CHOPPY, AND STEADILY INCREASING WAVES. BUT IT'S A TOUGH OLD BOAT. WE'RE COMING IN FROM THE SOUTH. THAT CLOUD SEEMS TO BE MOVING DOWN FROM THE NORTH. THIS IS FUN, A RACE TO THE LAUNCH. WE STILL HAVE A LONG WAY TO GO. I DON'T THINK THAT WE ARE GOING TO WIN.

SOME WAVES SEEM LIKE THEY WILL WASH COMPLETELY OVER THE BOAT. IT'S SO CHOPPY. WE CAN'T PICK UP ANY PATTERN TO THEM. THEY'RE COMING FROM EVERY DIRECTION. IT LOOKS LIKE WE'VE INDEED LOST THE RACE.

I KNOW THAT DAD IS SCARED LIKE ME, BUT HE WINKS AND YELLS, "WE'RE HAVING FUN NOW!"

THE OLD MOTOR CONTINUES TO SPIT AND SPUTTER, BUT KEEPS RUNNING. I DON'T KNOW HOW.

THAT LAST WAVE WASHES IN GALLONS OF WATER. THE GEAR IS STARTING TO FLOAT. WE'RE TRYING TO BAIL

USING OUR DRINKING CUPS. MORE WATER FLOWS IN AS A WAVE HITS US BROADSIDE. DAD TRIES TO KEEP THE NOSE INTO THE WAVES. BUT WE CAN'T TELL FROM WHICH WAY ARE THEY COMING? THE MOTOR FLUTTERS ONCE. THEN IT DOES IT AGAIN AND GOES SILENT. ALL I CAN HEAR IS THE WIND WHIPPING THROUGH MY EARS AND THE WAVES POUNDING THE SIDE OF THE BOAT. DAD TURNS AROUND, GRABS THE STARTER ROPE AND PULLS. IT DOESN'T START. HE PULLS AGAIN. NOTHING. ANOTHER WAVE STANDS US ON OUR SIDE. WE TRY TO HANG ON. THE NEXT WAVE FLIPS THE BOAT.

THAT'S THE LAST THING I REMEMBER. I WAKE UP AND SEE THAT I'M LAYING ON THE DECK OF SOME BIG BOAT. I SIT UP AND WATCH THIS MAN AND A LADY WORKING OVER DAD. HE'S ON HIS BACK NEXT TO ME. AFTER A FEW MINUTES HE THROWS UP ALL KINDS OF YUCKY WATER.

THE MAN IS LAUGHING AND GIVES A HIGH-FIVE TO THE LADY BECAUSE HE IS HAPPY THAT MY DAD IS GOING TO BE FINE. HE'S SMILING AT ME; THE LADY IS TOO. I KNOW THAT MY DAD IS OKAY. I'M GLAD.

I REMEMBER SEEING THE MAN BEFORE. HE WAS ON THE PIER THE DAY THAT LITTLE GIRL FELL OVER. I REMEMBER HIS LAUGH AND SMILE. I THINK HE'S ALWAYS AROUND WHEN KIDS ARE IN TROUBLE.

"You have got to be kidding me!" Steven shouts. "When did this happen; this past September? Do you know the kid's name? Why didn't the reporter inform the authorities?"

"Slow down, Steven. Yes, this September and the kid's name is David, David Walker. The reporter didn't put two and two together. Why would he? He didn't know anything about there being a chance of the hero being alive."

"Well, I can! I sure as hell can put two and two together and it adds up to ten to twenty years. I want you to reopen the case. I can't wait to tell Sunshine!" he excitedly says.

+ + + +

"Well, Baby, what do you think? Do you want to make the trip with me tomorrow to Navarre? We now have all the proof necessary to make an arrest stick. A missing persons report was never filed. Two eye witnesses identified him; we found all the necessary gear in his shop, and a record of a long cell phone call two days after the incident. It's circumstantial but good enough; plus, I bet they'll admit to it when pressed."

"He saved your life Steven; and mine. They are not bad people. You know it just like I do. That little girl; what happens to her? You saw the way they worship her and each other. Maggie was desperate to rid herself of that creep. She took special care to make sure no one would be harmed. Of course it was risky, but she did it to protect herself and her baby. I don't know that I wouldn't do the same thing if it were me," says Sunshine forcibly.

"She took a million and a half dollars. That's fraud, pure and simple. And they endangered Abby," he insists.

"No! To answer your question; I don't want to go with you."

"Suit yourself," he snaps back.

CHAPTER FIFTY-THREE

Eleven Months After The Incident
Monday, February 4, 2014 at 6:00 PM

The announcer on the six o'clock news informs his local viewers that the bizarre trial of a couple using their young daughter in a plan to defraud the State of Alabama by faking her murder is set to begin tomorrow morning. Continuing, he says, "The unimaginable scheme they concocted was to have someone drop her off a pier into the Gulf of Mexico. They are officially charged with attempted murder, endangering the life and limb of a child, plus several minor related offenses. The trial is expected to last at least a week unless a plea bargain can be reached."

+ + + +

"Maggie, did you hear that?" Rick calls outs.

"Yes, I heard. Can you please turn it down? I get so upset when I hear about it over and over again."

"Sure; no problem."

"I'm so frustrated. Our lives are in such chaos. They will be for a long time and we can't do anything about it. I know it's selfish, but I sometimes think it was wrong for me to ask you not to harm them. You should have let them both drown when you had the chance!"

"That's crazy talk! You know you don't mean that. The only thing we have going for us is the fact that I did return and pick them up," he retorts.

"You do have to admit, that if they were both gone, we'd be sitting on the beach in front of our paid-for condo as Mr. and Mrs. Rubio watching Abby build sand castles. Now, our castle is crumbling. . . . I wanted it all; Justin to be gone, you to be with me, and the money. I still do." she offers.

"Honey, you're frustrated. I understand that. So am I. But, it's time we decide what we're going to do when tomorrow morning comes around."

After a long period of silence, Maggie says, "It's all just so darn upsetting. It's finally and really sinking in that we are going to go to jail. It's just a matter of how many years, twenty-five or five. Even though all the evidence against us is circumstantial, it is a compelling case. I don't imagine there is much chance that we will be found innocent. People don't like people that put kids in harm's way. Abby will still be a little girl after five years but a grown woman after twenty-five. We were fortunate that our sweet neighbor with all those kids agreed to take her in. She'll be happy there. We were also lucky that child services approved of that arrangement as long as they can make frequent visits."

"Abby will be fine, but Maggie, are you saying that we should accept the plea?" he asks.

"I guess that's what I'm saying," she answers as she begins to cry.

"Rick holds her and they each sob uncontrollably."

+ + + +

Twenty minutes later Rick calls the lawyer and informs him of their decision. He tells Rick that he will inform the judge immediately and, in his experience, the sentence will be brought down within thirty to forty-five days.

CHAPTER FIFTY-FOUR

Eleven and One Half Months After The Incident
Monday, March 4, 2014 at 9:00 AM

Mrs. Margaret James Rubio is sentenced to ten years in prison with the possibility of parole after five, plus five years probation. She is ordered to repay the insurance funds to the state of Alabama; in full, plus interest.

Mr. Richard Rubio is sentenced to five years to be served in Navarre, Florida under house arrest, plus five years probation. An ankle bracelet allows him to work the shop.

Abigail James will reside with the neighbors. A review of this arrangement will be undertaken by the court within thirty months.

+ + + +

Under supervision, on the first Monday of each month, Rick takes Abby to visit Maggie.

Made in the USA
Columbia, SC
26 November 2017